GOSPEL
FOR THE
DAMNED

A NOVEL BY

GORDON GRAVLEY

I0728428

Gospel for the Damned

Copyright © 2013 by Gordon Gravley

All rights reserved.
No part of this book may be reproduced in any form or by any means,
electronic or mechanical, including photocopying, recording,
or any information storage and retrieval system,
without written permission from the author.

Gospel for the Damned is a work of fiction.
Names, characters, places, and incidents are products
of the author's imagination or are used fictitiously.
Any resemblance to actual events, locales, or persons,
living or dead, is entirely coincidental.

IngramSpark Paperback Edition

Published by GenreGamutBooks

ISBN-13: 978-1-948718-00-4

LCCN: 201-3900-417

Cover by Bespoke Book Covers

Subscribe to the author's newsletter
via his website gordongravley.com

To my wife, Jenna,

who I couldn't have made it this far without.

Contents

Gospel
for the
Damned

A THIN LINE

It was an opportunity that would make my career or crumble it, and I'd like to say it came to me by way of my diligence and journalistic talent. But truthfully, I was given the assignment for the simple reason that I was the only one on staff at the *Sound* who tested as resistant to the Omega virus; it was my luck to be in the 2 percent of the nation immune to a disease that, to date, had wiped out a third of the West Coast's population.

San Francisco was ground zero. As one of the few civilians, let alone journalists, allowed to enter the city limits since the quarantine was enacted two years prior, I was to spend three days interviewing the family of Samuel Elliot, a minister who had gone missing while under government surveillance, and the primary suspect responsible for the release of the Omega upon the Bay Area. There were other suspects, including the radical groups Shepherds of Prophecy and Mother One, but it was Samuel Elliot that the

FBI was most interested in.

My assignment, as stated by my editors, and the FBI, was to learn anything I could about the errant minister, anything at all that would lead to his whereabouts. And I was to do this, of course, without raising suspicion.

For myself, I wanted to report about life in the aftermath of a terrifying, nearly apocalyptic event from the perspective of those closest to the very individual supposed to have caused it. Also, what of the fractured communities whose future was doubtful at best? How would they live without hope? It was a story that would write itself, I thought; the imagery, the drama, the poignancy were all in place, waiting to be documented. The real challenge, I would discover, (besides staying alive) was maintaining an objective, uninvolved distance.

*   *   *

A complete physical and psychological exam was only the first of several checkpoints I would have to pass through before getting inside the city. I was given a mandatory colored ID bracelet—glowing green for "safe," or uninfected. (Orange indicated a significant metabolic change and that the wearer should be tested, while red meant infection.) The bracelet also had GPS capabilities for tracking patients and could be scanned for all pertinent personal information. I was also required to wear a visitor's badge and carry a half-inch-thick stack of notarized letters, health and psychiatric records, and multiple forms of identification that bulged from my jacket pocket with frumpish indignation. All of this, I believe, was to set me apart as an outsider; I didn't belong there. Thus, even with all the proper documentation, the motives of my presence were suspiciously scrutinized.

The judgments began at the airport, where I had to trudge through a mire of military green and incredulous looks. The soldiers, embittered from battling a resentful populace and criticisms of their own, didn't know what to think of me. It seemed only the obsessed and troubled would live so precariously. Who would willingly enter hell? I would, apparently. Corporal McDowell, my driver into the city, summarized the general disbelief when he said to me, "This is some kind of fetish you've got."

"I'm writing an article," I told him, looking to prove my lucidity.

"I hope you're getting paid well," he replied. Corporal McDowell was a youthful, imposing soldier who carried himself more like a general than a noncom. He made me feel vulnerable and frail.

"It's a rare opportunity. Once in a lifetime," I added.

"Let's hope it's not the last in a lifetime."

The corporal drove us in silence for a time. Then he said, "Forget about any pictures or footage you've seen of San Necropolis here. It's worse. We're in our own kind of Dark Ages."

I had arrived to the city with feelings of trepidation that only grew in response to the corporal's comment. Images I had seen throughout my research were nothing less than horrific: people plummeting to the bay waters from the barricaded Golden Gate and Bay Bridges in desperate attempts to leave the city; the brutal clash of civilians against one another, against the police, and against the military in riots that occurred for many long months; a priest's head being crushed beneath the wheels of a cable car. How could I forget any of that and expect the reality to be even worse?

Initially, the drive into the city did little to ease my burgeoning misgivings. I had arrived midmorning, and though the cloud cover was already burned off by the sun, there was grayness to the neighborhoods that bordered the clear highway. I felt we were shooting down a tunnel, plunging to foreboding depths. There were gauntlets of military checkpoints at every major exit off the freeway, and a couple directly on the 101—twice more I was subjected to disdainful leers and presumptuous questions by overworked National Guardsmen. The presence of Corporal McDowell, my official escort, did nothing to lessen the intensity of their examinations.

Then, as we drove on, heading west along Interstate 280, I peered out the Hummer's passenger-side window and began to settle into only a moderate queasiness. The shocking reality, of which the corporal had implied, surprisingly, began to subside. It was quiet and mournful, yes; menacing, barbaric, and out of control, no. I was encouraged further as we left I-280 by one of the few exits that was not also a checkpoint, wound through some residential neighborhoods, and ended up on Brotherhood Way. Corporal McDowell caught me staring at the sign—BROTHERHOOD—as we drove past.

"Irony and hope, eh?" he said.

I asked him why there were no soldiers at the exit.

"This area is secure," he replied. "For now."

I couldn't lie to myself. I knew it was quiet because of the vacant streets and homes. The area was lonesome; there was no denying the despair. Yet the drive through Ingleside with the occasional pedestrian or family outside was strangely heartening, and I held to that as the corporal began to summarize the rules and regulations regarding my three-day visit.

"You want to stay west of Van Ness Avenue and north of Market Street. Your booklet outlines more specific boundaries, but that's a good rule of thumb." The "booklet" he referred to was a 150-page manual I was given in Seattle, a little light reading for my flight, that covered the dos and don'ts of visiting this military restricted area. "You are obligated to contact us immediately if you feel your health and safety have been compromised in any way. Contact numbers are on the first page of your booklet. I know you've been tested and retested, but be aware that the Omega has mutated more than once. The best that physicians have been able to do is stay one step behind. Do you have any questions so far?"

"No," I answered. While he went on about curfews and other social restrictions, his voice became white noise—my attention was drawn to some passing graffiti-plastered billboards and fences. Amid the cryptic symbols and colorful profanity upon one wall, a concise, simple statement revealed itself:

GOD

HATES

COWARDS

The three words sliced through the October morning like a beacon. From a billboard down the road, another sentence emerged:

HOPE IS THE

FALLOUT OF DESPAIR

And then one more, a little farther along, upon the side of a San Francisco State University building, each letter as big as a person:

BE OUR

FUTURE'S PAST

As I copied them into my Moleskine notebook, the sound of my own name broke my concentration.

"Mr. Garrett?" Corporal McDowell repeated.

"Yes? I'm sorry?"

"The curfew is twenty-one hundred hours, not nineteen hundred as it states in your booklet."

"Nine o'clock?"

"Yes. And we are very diligent about our patrols, so

please be sure that you are indoors to stay by that time. Curfew lifts at oh-six-hun...six a.m. Do you have any questions at this time?"

"No."

"And stay away from the parade."

"The parade?"

"We're now entering the Sunset District."

As the corporal had stated earlier, the city was divided. There were areas that were secure—that is, deemed virus-free—and those that remained infectious. Due to the nature of the Omega's dispersion—a series of aerosol bombs set off in the northeastern part of the city, primarily the Financial District—it was difficult to initially isolate the virus. Only through quarantine of the entire city, use of the federal euthanasia and disposal program, and the locking down of neighborhoods, one by one, into "safe" and "bio-threat" sections was containment truly possible. While boundaries changed daily, for the most part, the divisions were clear. The Sunset District, in the southwestern corner of the city, had been the first area to be secured.

There, a few blocks from the zoo, in a small three-bedroom shoebox tucked tightly within rows and rows of shoeboxes, lived the Elliot family. Their dingy, pastel home was indiscernible from the rest. Corporal McDowell drove directly to it; he had obviously been there before.

People were out for strolls in the crisp air; children were playing. On the front steps of the Elliot home sat a young man in his early to mid-teens. His short, dark hair framed a pair of bright, optimistic eyes; I wasn't sure whether to take him as genuine or daft. He, like those on the street and everyone who lived in the area, wore a green wristband like mine. The corporal wished me luck and drove off, leaving me with the exuberant teenager.

From my research, I knew the Elliot family as Samuel, Emily, and their sons—Zachary, age twenty, and Benjamin, fourteen. I took the teenager on the steps to be Benjamin. I also knew him from his blog *The Thin Line*, which he wrote for six weeks just prior to the city's quarantine. As he came down the steps to greet me, I recalled his first posting: "If there's ever to be an end of days, I think we're living it now, here, in my life."

"Mr. Garrett?" he said. "I'm Ben Elliot."

"Hello, Ben. Call me Aaron."

He grabbed my bag with ease (strong for his size) and led me up the nine or ten tiled steps to the front door. Before entering the house, I paused a moment to take in the tranquil autumn glow—only to find I had an audience. Neighbors and passersby had gathered to see the anomaly, the fetish-beset visitor. I gave a cordial nod and went inside, thinking, perhaps, that I was the daft one for being there.

The front door creaked open, and I was hit with the warm aroma of a home too small for the number of people living in it and windows shut tight to keep out the October chill. The interior was bright with light—no apparent concerns for energy conservation. In the living room sat two women. One had Ben's eyes, and she clutched a yellowed, tattered Bible. She introduced herself as Mrs. Elliot. The other woman—frail and withdrawn—did nothing to acknowledge my presence. Instead, she gazed zombielike into a television, her face inches from its screen.

Mrs. Elliot stood and, taking my hands, welcomed me into her home. Before I knew it, I was telling her all about myself: growing up in Seattle, my family scattering about the country, working at the *Sound*. Even my favorite childhood pet, a mutt of a dog named Spatz, entered the conversation. I wondered whom this stranger who looked like me was, opening up so easily to the minister's wife.

There was a teenage girl sitting in a corner of the room, as engrossed in her e-book as the frail woman was with her television. Considering her black, fuchsia-streaked hair, I was surprised I hadn't seen her when I first entered. She looked up at me, revealing delicate Asian features and hard eyes, and then she quickly resumed her reading.

"That's Nikki in the corner," Mrs. Elliot said, "and you've met my son, Ben. This is Mrs. Miller, but don't mind her, she keeps to herself. Ben, could you show Mr. Garrett where he can put his things?"

Ben took my bag once again, and I followed him from the living room into the hall. "Dane and Nikki share that room," he pointed out. "That's Peter's room. He's in there working right now. He's a licensed net agent for Harrison

Telecom. You'll be down here with me and Zac."

The room at the end of the hall was tiny and made even more so with the addition of a third bed—or cot, that is. I asked Ben about the others living in the house.

"Peter, Dane, and Nikki are friends of ours."

"And Mrs. Miller?"

"She's Peter's mother. She sleeps in his room. Otherwise, she watches TV. Zac's working a lunch shift, so you can have the room to yourself to settle in, if you want."

I sat down on my cot and looked around the windowless room. For the most part, it was a boy's room: clothes hanging on chairs and doorknobs; shoes stuffed under beds; more sports paraphernalia and magazines than books; a pile of electronic games stashed in the closet, which I imagined hadn't been played in a while, not since the brothers had become too old to admit they liked such things; and an array of indiscernible teenage clutter, like a high school's lost-and-found bin.

One item did catch my attention—an outdated shortwave radio, similar to one I had when I was Ben's age that I had inherited from my grandfather. It was curious to see such an antiquated method of broadcasting. Perhaps it was a mere curio for the boys, a piece of junk dug out of the trash. Or was it a memento like the one I'd had handed down by a relative? I leaned in for a closer look and heard voices. Faraway words from the other side of the world? No, more like the muffled conversation of people on the other side of the wall.

I jumped at Ben's entrance. With the look of a puppy having spied its owner, he said, "You should come out and meet Dane! She works for the FCO[†]."

From the hallway, I saw two new people to meet—a man and a woman— standing in the living room. The man had a clean, unassuming look; bland, without expression. He nearly disappeared within the small group collected there. The woman was short and fit; her hair was ratty and unkempt, but there was a certain appeal to her unruliness. While the name "Dane" had seemed a bit androgynous to me at first, I suspected right away that, of the two of them standing there, *she* was the object of Ben's enthusiasm. (I also knew that I was making an assumption about his sexual preference as I extended my hand to her.)

"You must be Dane," I said.

Her grip was confident and her stare unwavering in its judgment as she replied, "And you must be the reporter come to spy on us."

"I'm just here to observe and learn."

Though I was there by invitation of Mrs. Elliot, I would have to earn all of their trust. I had to admit, their suspicions were warranted, much more so than those of the soldiers and the neighbors upon my arrival. The moment Samuel Elliot had dropped out of the government's radar, their lives were turned inside out. Their home was torn apart amid a search

---

[†] Federal Coroner's Office

for clues to his whereabouts, and everyone living there was taken into custody and pummeled with questions for days, until lawyers finally intervened. For their own protection, Feds wanted to move the family to a safe house, but Mrs. Elliot declined. "We've done nothing wrong and have nothing to hide," she'd stated.

When a barrage of requests came for an interview from the media, Mrs. Elliot, again saying they had "nothing to hide," did agree to a story on the condition that the chosen journalist came to their home in person. She also insisted it not be a reporting institution like the *New York Times* or the *Washington Post*—she didn't trust them. "They're too desperate to stay in print. It will cloud their judgment," she'd explained. Thus, a small yet respected Northwest-based online news source and a relatively inexperienced site designer and writer were chosen to learn her family's side of the story.

Dane kept her grip upon my hand a bit longer in her assessment of me. Once satisfied—with my character? my integrity? my hand strength?—she released her hold and introduced me to the unassuming Peter Miller, the net agent and son of the woman fixated upon the television.

"We're going out to lunch," she then said, meaning her, Peter, Ben, and Nikki. "You should join us."

Mrs. Elliot saw my hesitation and said, "She's right. We'll have plenty of time to talk."

"You said you wanted to learn something," Dane added.

I was soon outside, with the four of them describing to me how, after all that had happened, San Francisco still had the best public transit system in the country. "It's even better," said Dane with a wry grin, "now that there aren't a ton of passengers clogging it up."

Nikki laughed, but that didn't hide her apprehension to being outside. The others assured her we would not be leaving any clean zones. "The buses don't go anywhere else, anyway," said Dane. Nikki's anxiety made her much more vocal and animated than when we'd met at the house; she and Dane prattled away like sisters.

Within minutes of reaching the bus stop, we caught the Sunset Line that would take us through a neighborhood or two before its straight shot up Nineteenth Avenue. Our destination: the reopening of Flynn's Fish 'n' Chips, just three blocks from Golden Gate Park. The reopening of anything was an event, one of many steps toward what I would find to be the elusive goal of normalcy.

Ben was beaming as he peered out a window, and Peter couldn't stop going on about the exceptional battered halibut he would be enjoying.

"It's the only fishy taste you'll ever experience," commented Dane with her hooked smile.

"Get shredded," replied Peter.

The amount of activity on the streets was equivalent to a small rural town. Traffic moved along smoothly because, well, there really wasn't any, and there were so few pedestrians that I could imagine knowing them all by name. I sighted only a couple military vehicles; there was not much need for them in that part of the city at that time of the day.

I didn't know what to make of the blue sky as we drove past empty homes and schools and boarded-up storefronts. It didn't seem right that I should enjoy the day, knowing full well why those buildings were vacant and closed; I didn't feel it was my place to make jokes. The four of them were allowed—and expected—to grasp moments of beauty or humor, but the same thing from me just seemed cynical and rude.

Upon one of the boarded windows, I read:

A THIN LINE

DEFINES NORMAL

The Thin Line *is the name of Ben's blog,* I thought to myself. A coincidence? I turned to ask them about the message, as well as the others I had seen, but I was interrupted by Nikki asking Dane, "What color?"

Dane looked at a passing speed limit sign and responded, "Reddish-orange."

Ben pointed to a billboard with black lettering.

"Mauve," Dane answered.

"Mauve?" Ben shot back. "What's that? That's not a color."

As they laughed, I had to ask what they were doing.

"It's a game we play," said Ben.

"I have a condition," Dane explained with a shrug.

"Synaesthesia. My senses merge, and I see colors with sounds, or letters will have colors when they really don't."

"I've heard of it," I told her.

We got off the bus near Judah Street and walked a few blocks to the restaurant, where a line down the block was waiting to partake of Flynn's deep-fried fare. It didn't matter that it was going to be a forty-five-minute wait. There was a consensual patience and courtesy between everyone in line because being outside on such a beautiful day was the real treat; welcoming a business back into the neighborhood—the communal equivalent to a barn raising—was as good a reason as any to be out of doors.

Mr. Cheng, aka "Flynn," came out to greet us while we waited and offer samples—fried salmon with his own tangy dipping sauce as well as his sublime fried mac 'n' cheese. His small body was out of proportion with his overly round head, and he had a rambunctious laugh that triggered a similar response in others. He had plenty of reasons to smile, as his was one of only three other businesses in the immediate vicinity, sharing the block with a Laundromat and a corner convenience store.

Once inside, waiting at the counter for our order, I thought to play the color game with Dane. I pointed up at the menu on the wall and asked her, "What color is coleslaw?"

She grinned and looked up. "Red. The first couple letters of each item is red."

"Not all the letters?"

"No, but that's the way it usually is, just the first few letters of a group, like a word or sentence."

"That one?" I asked, referring to a CASH ONLY sign next to her.

"C-A-S is aquamarine."

A number of people were getting their meals to go, and I suggested we do the same, with the close proximity of Golden Gate Park. Everyone agreed, and it wasn't long before we were sitting on cool grass, not too far into the park, in the light of the warming sun.

For the moment, I just wanted to observe and enjoy my lunch. Dane, Nikki, and Peter talked about some of the cute men who were standing in line with us. Ben griped about how boring some of his classes had been, Introduction to Logic in particular. (At the time of this writing, attending school was done entirely online.) Then, together, the four of them reminisced about past afternoons spent there at the park, before the plague. Afterward, taking (sadly) my last bite, I mentioned that I wanted to see more of the city.

"I can show you around," Ben said. "I know all the bus routes."

The others were heading back home; Dane and Peter had to go to work, and Nikki needed to get indoors. With the tone of a big sister, Dane cautiously consented to Ben accompanying me.

"Don't forget about curfew," Nikki reminded us.

"Be home long before that, or you're screwed," said

Dane.

Under his breath, Ben vented his displeasure at Dane playing the role of big sister.

I followed Ben at a quick pace to a bus line that would take us through the Presidio and then to the Marina District. There was more of the same cityscape from earlier: sparse traffic, boarded-up buildings, people making their best efforts toward business as usual.

"Doesn't the city look like an exhibit at some kind of history museum?" Ben said. "Except, one that's under construction—you know, incomplete. Look, there's a backdrop of the Golden Gate Bridge. And here's a reproduction of the Palace of Fine Arts. Look at the detail!"

"There is something unreal about it," I added and gestured to a couple strolling down a pristine stretch of sidewalk, then said, "Paid performers or automatons?"

One glance at the couple's distant expressions of indifference and he replied, "Oh, automatons for sure!"

We transferred to another bus that would take us closer to some restricted areas. Almost immediately, there were even fewer people on the streets. There were also a number of buildings that weren't exactly boarded up, but were barricaded for limited access. I asked Ben about them.

"It means someone living there tested positive for the virus," he explained. "That's what Dane does for the FCO. If just one person is positive, the whole building is quarantined, and everyone inside has to be tested."

"Then what happens?"

"The positives can always opt for elective release," Ben stated very matter-of-factly.

"Elective release? You mean euthanasia, right?"

"Yes. Otherwise, they are moved to a restricted area. If enough people are infected, then they redefine the neighborhood as unclean and barricade the streets. Like that!" He pointed ahead as we approached Van Ness Avenue. We got off at the next stop and walked to the intersection. Ben advised that we didn't loiter or walk along Van Ness for too long. "We shouldn't go more than a couple of blocks," he said.

Along the center of the avenue ran a wall of concrete slabs, ten feet or more in height, topped with barbed wire fencing and much of its cold, gray surface covered by government signage—warnings and regulations—and graffiti. I looked up and down the street. Every few intersections, I could see, was a military checkpoint, gaps in the wall, to allow access for service vehicles and personnel.

Soldiers patrolled the sectioned lengths of wall, back and forth. No businesses were open; only a random few civilians were around, gawking like Ben and me, until a soldier asked them to move along. No longer were the romantic images of the city by the bay, but a scene more reminiscent of any war zone from the past century.

Ben pulled me off the avenue at the second intersection we came to. "I know where we can catch a bus," he said.

When we reached the stop, he asked, "Could you not mention to anyone when we get back that we came out this far? Especially Dane."

"Of course," I assured him. Then I asked, "What happens to anyone found negative in a building full of positives?"

"They're put into isolation, and retested, and retested. Kind of like Nikki, but her circumstances are different, actually."

We ended up riding a few different routes back, passing the Japanese Cultural Center and the University of San Francisco (only its administrative offices occupied), before heading all the way to the Pacific Ocean, where we got off the bus for a view of Seal Rock, a natural habitat for sea lions. We sat on a boulder and watched the ocean breathe its waves in and out over the sand.

"This is a favorite spot of mine," he said. "I like to see the planet as this huge living thing that we are only a small part of. Nothing that we do matters to it, really. Living or being sick or dying is all the same."

"Love and humanity, too?"

"None of it matters in the big picture. Only for the moment we are here. But that's okay," Ben replied with a content shrug.

Spoken like a minister's son, it occurred to me, peacefully resolved in deferring to something beyond his control, something greater than himself. I leaned back on the boulder and watched the ocean with him. There *was* comfort in its vastness and permanence. The two of us sat there for a time before realizing we were also watching a storm roll in over the setting sun. We needed to get home.

On the bus, I asked Ben, "Did you go to that spot with your father a lot?"

"No, that's my spot," he replied. He looked out his window at the coming twilight. We had lost track of the time in our respite on the beach; I wondered if he was concerned what Dane would do. Eventually, he said, "My father used to take me out with him all the time. Both me and Zac, but mostly me. Don't tell Zac, though. I don't think he always knew."

"Did your father have a different relationship with you than he did with your brother?"

"I guess so," Ben said with a fidget. "I helped him out with the church a lot more than Zac did."

I could see Ben was uncomfortable. We spent the remainder of the bus ride in silence. I had been in the city for only a few hours and experienced so much more than I had expected. But then, I had arrived not really knowing what to expect. I especially didn't think I would spend time on a rock, inhaling the sea wind and reflecting upon humankind's place in the universe. It was time well spent.

And to think, I spent it in San Necropolis.

*   *   *

Ben and I arrived at the house moments before Dane. She

came through the door with to-go containers of pizza and salad, and in tow, a towering, dread-headed man in his early twenties. She introduced us to her new partner—as in coworker—Quigley Mason. He had a dancing gaze, a car salesman's smirk, and he rocked back and forth in his stance, restless, as though about to run a sprint. He was so pressurized, in fact, that he had his own release valve, a kind of vocal tic, a noise that can best be represented onomatopoeically as *mmrp*. The two of them were in between shifts, so they had stopped to pick up dinner.

Restaurants hadn't been the most thriving businesses in the city since the quarantine. The few kitchens that did survive now operated under the toughest health codes, thus making their meals safer than anything you could prepare at home. Zachary, Mrs. Elliot's eldest son, was a prep cook and aspiring chef at The Cliff House, an icon of the city that had survived more than its share of disasters. Normally, he would bring home dinner, but Dane explained how she had received a call from him asking her to pick up something to eat that night.

"He's working late again?" Mrs. Elliot noted. "That's a good sign for business."

"I don't know. He just said he was going to be late," replied Dane flatly.

In the tradition of communal bonding over the breaking of bread (or in this case, an extra-large pepperoni-and-mushroom pizza), we gathered around the table, ate, and shared a bit of our histories. Actually, it was Mrs. Elliot who did most of the sharing about each of us as she thankfully recounted everyone's individual circumstances that had brought us together that evening. She considered everyone's presence there a godsend for which she was forever grateful.

It was not a matter of mere economic survival that all of them crowded into that small house—with plenty of prime real estate for cheap around the city, anyone could live comfortably on their own. Their cohabitation was for emotional survival; there were holes in their lives that could only be filled by the company of others.

According to Mrs. Elliot, "They were all friends in school. Zachary and Peter have known each other...how long?"

"Since second grade," answered Peter.

The girls came along in junior high. Ben fell in with the group because he and his brother were close—and because all his own friends had died. Zachary's love of cooking led him to The Cliff House, while Peter pursued a degree in Internet commerce to satisfy his want of financial security.

Dane left school to work at an animal hospital. It was because of her immunity status and experience as a veterinary technician that she was "recruited" for the Federal Coroner's Office as a civil attendant. Originally set up to simply deal with disposal of the deluge of corpses, the FCO had become a critical element in the containment of the disease.

While the rest of us sat at the table, Peter was on the couch with his mother, Jacqueline, holding her hand as she ate. Gauging by his twentysomething age, I guessed her to be in her early to mid-forties; however, she really looked much older. He had moved them both into the house to get her away from his father.

"It hasn't been long since she was able to feed herself," commented Mrs. Elliot as she observed me studying the two of them.

"I saw her go the bathroom on her own the other day," added Nikki.

Mrs. Elliot smiled. "That's wonderful."

Nikki sat next to me. She was reserved in making eye contact with the rest of us, even when speaking directly to us. She became part of the household after being separated from her family during one of the first riots that had occurred.

Between Dane and Mrs. Elliot sat Quigley Mason, his long legs stuffed under the table, one foot tapping away anxiously. That night was he and Dane's first shift together. Dane appeared strangely charmed by his intermittent *mmrps*. Being naturally curious, I couldn't help but ask him about his tic. Was it a form of Tourette's syndrome or part of an obsessive-compulsive disorder? Dane gave me a scornful glare because of the way her partner nervously cleared his throat a few times and ignored my inquiries.

Nibbling at a small serving of salad, Quigley also resisted Mrs. Elliot's pleas to fill up on as much as he wanted. When he explained he was a vegetarian, she promptly piled his plate with more greens. And then, as she had done with me, Mrs. Elliot lovingly proceeded to coax his life story from him.

Quigley was an only child from Los Angeles. He played the drums. He was also a painter and had moved north to attend the San Francisco Art Institute just before the plague. When the school was closed, he concluded that his painting—and all art—was irrelevant. He'd had an opportunity to safely leave before the quarantine. (LA hadn't been nearly as devastated by the Omega as San Francisco.) Instead, he chose to stick around and help.

"Is that when you were brought into the FCO?" Mrs. Elliot asked him.

"Actually, I sort of volunteered," Quigley answered, "almost a year ago. I didn't even know my immunity status at the time."

Mrs. Elliot considered what he'd said for a moment. "That's a position the average person doesn't normally gravitate to," she replied. Then, nodding her approval, she concluded, "It takes someone of a certain character to volunteer for such work."

"Or a crazy person," said Nikki.

Quigley began in the FCO as part of the Bearer Unit— those assigned to collect the heaps of bodies from all over the city and haul them to the crematorium.

"What was that like?" I asked him.

"Gruesome," he said, "especially trying to stuff them into bags after they've been dead a few days. But—*mmrp*—I got used to it. You learn to disconnect—*mmrp*—then I got promoted to the crematorium."

"After that, you were *demoted* to the streets," commented Dane.

"No, I don't think of it like that—*mmrp*. I asked for this assignment. Assisting others to a peaceful end is a worthwhile duty."

"Can you tell it's his first night?" Dane said, looking around at everyone.

"Have you given anyone a blue dream yet?" Nikki asked Quigley.

"He'll just be assisting me for a while," interjected Dane with a tone that suggested an impatience for work-related conversations. Then she stood and said, "I'm going to take Quig for a walk, show him the neighborhood before we head back out."

"Can I go with? It's not curfew yet," Ben chirped.

"Sure. We won't be gone long."

As Mrs. Elliot watched them leave, she said to me, "We've maintained a fairly normal life, don't you think? Not the social chaos you expected?"

"As much as I've seen so far," I told her. "I am surprised."

Mrs. Elliot looked past me to the couch. "Peter, dear, how's your mother doing?" she asked. The two of them had so little presence that I had forgotten they were there. Seeing Peter sitting with such calm and confidence made me think that he chose to go unnoticed, as though carrying out a clearly devised plan that involved no one but him and his mother.

"She's doing well, Mrs. Elliot," he answered. "We're just going to watch a little more before bed, if that's okay?"

"Of course it is."

Mrs. Elliot began to clear the dishes and silverware—the communal bonding was apparently over.

My place at the table had a good vantage point to see the rest of the room. None of the furniture appeared new, and the carpet needed to be replaced, but I'm sure redecorating was the furthest from anyone's mind. The walls were bare of paintings, prints, or photographs. There was a ceiling-high bookshelf sparse of books, and in a corner to my left was a set of low shelves with at least a dozen family photographs placed in a balanced, symmetrical formation that gave it the somber appearance of a shrine rather than a collection of fond memories. I moved to investigate the photographs and noticed Nikki had left the table to return to her reading. Peter was also up, leading his mother to their room. Before entering the hall, he turned to me with a nod to his mother. "She's not your story," he stated clearly.

I hesitated, unsure how to respond.

"Promise me," he said, "you won't tell her story."

"Okay. I promise," I told him.

The two of them retired to their room. As I leaned in for a closer look of the family pictures, Dane, Quigley, and Ben burst in from outside, drenched and laughing. Ben stated the obvious with, "We got rained on!" Still laughing, he went to the hall closet and grabbed towels for them to dry off. After a brief toweling, Dane and Quigley left us. Apparently, civil attendants with the FCO were exempt from the curfew, as it was nearly nine o'clock.

Mrs. Elliot returned, sitting down with a fresh cup of tea. Though not a small woman, her movements had a lovely grace, and I could've listened to her smooth, soothing voice for hours. She did enjoy telling a story.

"What brought you to San Francisco?" I asked her. (In my research, I had read that she grew up in Gresham, Oregon, born Emily Marie Grayson.)

"A job opportunity," she said. "I had just graduated nursing school, and there was more work available down here at the time. It was also a good chance to get out and see someplace new."

"That was how she met Dad," piped in Ben.

Mrs. Elliot wrapped a large, gentle arm around him, ran a hand through his damp hair, and gave him a kiss. "Yes, I met my husband on the highway. He assisted me when my car broke down."

"Your knight in shining armor," said Nikki with dreamy cynicism.

"More like greasy overalls. He had a mobile automotive

repair service, drove a midsize moving truck loaded with tools and spare parts. When business was slow, he would roam the roadways looking for stranded motorists. That's how he found me."

"Was it love at first sight?" I asked.

"Not until he didn't charge me for the labor." She gave a gentle laugh, then said, "I had a pretty good feeling about him after he escorted me into the city. Once I got settled, we began dating."

"What was he like?" I asked.

"You look like you could use a hot chocolate," she said to Ben, who responded with a grin. From the kitchen, she asked, "Mr. Garrett, would you like some tea or something?"

"Hot chocolate sounds great, actually. And call me Aaron, please."

Nikki gave a *psst* and directed me to the corner shelf unit of photographs. "He's the one with red hair and the Rasputin gaze," she said.

I went to the corner for a closer look.

There he was, in a snapshot within a green cardboard frame, standing on a beach of gray sand with the ocean barely visible through a fogbank. Nikki was right: his eyes were wide, spellbinding, and not exactly optimistic; rather, they possessed a deep fervor, religious or otherwise. Though he was alone in the picture, it was easy to see his height; he was even taller than Quigley, I guessed, and he was topped off by a head of messy orange-red hair.

"For the most part, he was a peaceful man," Mrs. Elliot said. "Not some crazed mystical leader. He had his moments, of course, like a speed bump on a smooth road." She stood behind me, sharing my view of her husband's image.

"What kind of 'speed bumps'?"

"He could lash out, verbally. Not at anyone or anything in particular. He would just snap, like he'd finally had enough. An instant later, he would be himself."

"He used to joke that he was just shouting over the voices in his head," added Ben.

"Do you think he really did hear voices?" I asked.

"He was impassioned, emotional," said Mrs. Elliot. "There was no doubt in Samuel. He was confident in his convictions, like no one I've ever known. He made you believe because he believed. Sometimes, those convictions were overwhelming. I think that is what he heard."

Among the old-fashioned print photographs was a digital frame containing a series of interchanging pictures. There were shots of Samuel beside different incarnations of his moving truck: in its original form as a touring auto repair shop and then in its later version as a mobile church (not that you could tell from the outside—it would be something I would learn later). In other photos, he stood in front of a building that was his first church; though it was a plain single-floor construct, he glowed with such enthusiasm for it.

With a cup of warming hot chocolate in hand, I perused other pictures. In one, the brothers wrestled at a picnic in the park; in another, they raced along the ocean shore. There was another with father and sons posing like statues before the De Young Museum. My favorite, though, had Samuel apparently giving the boys a lesson in juggling. A pair of pinecones and a handball-size rock was frozen precariously in the air between them. Their father teetered like a drunken clown as Ben watched, awestruck, and Zac braced himself for the predictable outcome.

There, in that assortment of memories, was that "normal life" Mrs. Elliot had spoken of earlier. The genuine happiness and normalcy in those pictures conflicted with what Ben had shown me that afternoon, like the wall dividing Van Ness Avenue. Lying upon my cot hours later, unable to sleep, I had some difficulty wrapping my head around the concepts of quarantine and curfew. Not being allowed to go where you wanted, anytime you wanted, unable to leave your house—those were the oppressive realities of other countries, not America. Those kinds of things just didn't happen here. Certainly, government control was for our own protection, and each action had its purpose—the quarantine contained the spread of the virus, and curfew helped keep the peace—but I could not align it with any definition I had of a regular life. I was sinking into an uneasy sensation of walking that thin line between normal and everything else.

UNNATURAL BEHAVIOR

It was after midnight when a noise from the kitchen stirred me from my cot. With Ben asleep next to me, I got up to see who it was. In the living room, Mrs. Elliot slept in her chair, and at the kitchen table, attacking the leftover pizza, sat Zachary Elliot, the eldest son. Like Quigley Mason, Zac had nervous energy, his sinewy muscles twitching. Unlike Quigley, though, he lacked confidence; his handshake was a little too firm as he introduced himself.

"Call me Aaron," I replied.

"Want some pizza?" he asked, pointing to the last slice.

I declined and sat down at the table with him.

After finishing that remaining piece in what appeared to be a single bite, barely chewing and gulping it down whole, Zac asked me questions about my work and what I thought of the city. His speech was rapid and loud. I glanced over to Mrs. Elliot, who snored lightly just a few feet from us.

"My mother could sleep through an earthquake," he said, waving off my concern.

"How is it working at The Cliff House?" I asked in a hushed tone, hoping to calm his jitters.

"I'm lucky to be working at all. And then to be working *there*?"

Dane came in the front door just then. She looked dazed, emotionally spent; her body slumped from the weight of a long day. I felt tired just looking at her. She wished me a good night but said nothing to Zac on her way to her room. Before going in, she stopped at the door and said, "You should go to work with me tomorrow, if you really want to learn something."

"Okay," I told her.

I turned back to Zac. "Do you often put in late hours, like tonight?"

"Ever since the post-curfew shuttle service was set up, we get customers that like to show their money with big parties and late nights." Zac's wavering gaze settled upon the empty pizza box between us, and he went quiet.

"Maybe it's their way of feeling in control of an uncontrollable situation," I said.

"I guess," Zac sighed. He rubbed his eyes, not so much to soothe them, but rather, it seemed, to erase a thought or image from his mind. Then—snap!—with a grin, he said, "I need a walk."

"A walk? Now?"

"You should come out with me. I can show you some things."

Naturally, I hesitated. "But…It's almost one, well after curfew."

"That's only an issue if you get caught, and we won't get caught. Besides, there aren't many patrols around this part of town."

"You don't think you might be under surveillance?"

Zac shrugged and said, "It's not like we're going to go meet my father or anything."

Having seen Dane's fatigue, all I wanted at that moment was to fall back onto my little cot and sleep, yet the taboo of going out was enticing. There was plenty of time for rest later.

"Sure. Let's go," I said.

Zac was already standing at the opened front door, gazing into the black of night beyond. A rush of damp air, brisk with the smell of the Pacific, rolled into the house and across our feet. It was exhilarating, and it lured me to stand with him and observe how the darkness of the street engulfed the light from the living room, as I knew it was about to engulf both of us.

"It's quiet," I said.

"Quiet is good, right?" Zac said and stepped out. It was more than quiet as we went down to the sidewalk—it was desolate, with the only prevalent sound coming from trash blown along the asphalt by a night breeze. I paused to listen carefully and heard the comforting whisper of the ocean in the distance. Waiting at the corner, Zac looked in every direction and then started down another block.

"Where are we going?" I asked him.

"You don't have to go with me if you don't want," he replied as he kept walking.

"It's not that," I said. (I had to admit, there was a thrill about being out—the absence of four secure walls, concrete beneath my feet.) "I just want to know where we're going."

"To the zoo," he said.

Many of the streetlights were out, either damaged by vandals—evident by the crunch of shattered glass under our steps—or simply from neglect due to a scarcity of city maintenance workers. Whatever illumination there was came mostly from porch lights or the occasional glow from a curtained window. The curtains stayed closed, though; we were unwatched and alone. Turning a corner that brought the zoo into our sight, the two of us passed a lot where the blackened, skeletal framework and fallen sections of stucco wall were all that remained of whatever had once stood there.

"What happened here?" I wondered aloud.

"It was some kind of community center," Zac answered. "It burned down months ago."

We eventually reached Sloat Boulevard, and Zac said, "Hurry!"

Following his lead, I ran across the wide street and slid to a stop before scrunching down within the shadows of overgrown bushes that lined the sidewalk and bordered the zoo grounds. As Zac began to creep eastward along the walkway, I pointed out that the entrance was in the opposite direction.

"We can't get in that way," he said in a forced whisper. "It's guarded."

"Guarded? By whom and from what?"

"By the residents, from everyone else."

We crept along, careful to remain in the shadows, for a laughably long distance. I investigated our immediate vicinity, up and down the boulevard, finding no one else anywhere. "Can't we just walk?" I asked.

Zac stopped, thrust a hand up to hush me, and listened. Satisfied he didn't hear anything, he responded with a sharp "No."

So on we crept.

Eventually, we came to a bare spot in the untended landscaping. Zac looked around once again and then wriggled inside. I followed him into a low, narrow swath within the otherwise dense foliage. The soil was cold and damp with a distinct moldy, mushroom aroma. Feeling claustrophobic, I focused on the soles of his shoes, his feet scooting along as he crawled in front of me. I could feel we were squeezing under a fence or a wall, but it was too dark to be sure, and I was clueless of the moment we transitioned from our hole into an open grassy area surrounded by trees. It wasn't until Zac stood that I realized.

He took careful steps toward a tree in front of us and

crouched next to it; I stood behind him, well hidden from whatever was on the other side. Peering around the trunk, I saw a paved pathway, the blackened forms of a few small buildings, what appeared to be a number of vacant animal exhibits, and then some yurts and tents—lots of tents. Zac tugged on my sleeve, and I knelt beside him.

"People live here," he said. "And they don't like visitors."

"Then what are we doing here?" I asked.

"I want to show you something."

With that, he stepped onto the path and began to walk, casually. I followed his lead, yet I was anything but casual with all my senses on overdrive and my heart racing.

"Try to look like you're supposed to be here," Zac told me, "like you're one of them. And pull your sleeve over your bracelet. Cover it up."

"Okay," I said warily. "Exactly who are these people?"

"They're homeless," he replied. "This started as a tent city, right after it was closed down and the animals were transported out. As it got crowded, they cleaned up some exhibits and shelters and moved into them. Families with seniors or children live in the offices or the gift shop, wherever it's warm."

Among the yurts and tents were other, cruder shelters, like lean-tos and tarps strung between trees. Many were dimly lit by lanterns and flashlights and occupied by silhouetted figures. As we moved along toward the center of the complex, I heard conversation and laughter and saw light from buildings ahead of us.

"The city agreed to keep the power and water on for them, as long as they stayed here," Zac continued. "Food, clothes, and other essentials are donated. They've built a real community. They don't leave, and nobody comes in. That's why it's the cleanest part of town—you know, virus-free."

"If they were allowed to live in abandoned housing within the city, they might be more susceptible," I surmised.

"Exactly. It's all about containment. Besides, the city's going to make a fortune on real estate when it's time to rebuild. And when the zoo is ready to return, all these folks will be back on the streets. Everything back to normal, that's the goal, right?"

The path we followed led us to the lion house. Lights were on inside, and people socialized within, gathering around tables of food and drink; with Halloween only days away and appropriate decorations accenting the interior, it was their own fall festival. I noticed, especially, how no one appeared desperate or destitute, and the children, mostly in costume and excited to be staying up so late, looked healthy and happy. A group of them surrounded an old woman whose gray-streaked hair was tied so tight in a bun that she appeared to be wearing a formfitting hat. I couldn't quite make out the story she told them—something about the history of Halloween and its pagan lineage—but she told it with great enthusiasm.

Except for the barred cages big enough to house a pride

of lions along two sides of the spacious indoors, it could have been a potluck party in any community hall of any borough in any city. A few mingled just outside the entrances and paid no attention to the two of us as we strolled past.

Zac diverted me from there to an empty exhibit on the far side of the building and directed my attention to a wall where a stretch of graffiti ran its length. There was just enough ambient light from the lion house for me to make out the words:

UNNATURAL BEHAVIOR

IS FAILURE

"I saw a message like this on my way into the city—several, in fact," I said.

Zac responded with nothing but a cocky, knowing smirk.

"Did you do this?" I asked him.

"No," he said and laughed. "But I know who did. Come on, there's more this way."

The next stop was a flight of concrete stairs that were a part of the primate discovery center. Along one wall was written:

SURVIVING IS

NOT LIVING

We climbed the steps to the upper level, which had been designed to give zoo-goers a view of the inhabitants existing, as they would have in nature, in an elevated environment. At one time, some of the world's most endangered species of primates roamed those exhibits: howler monkeys, siamangs, lion-tailed macaques, and emperor tamarins. But at that moment, they were occupied by a few homeless—and equally endangered?—teenagers, using the exhibit as a playground. They chased each other, laughed, and hung from tree limbs and ropes, unaware that Zac and I watched from above.

I felt awkward gawking at them, so I wandered away and viewed, instead, the sight of the zoo grounds permeated by the night like a thick fog. The glow of the various facilities and lights from the less permanent "homes" dotted and shaped the area, creating the appearance of a city all its own. I felt an air of calm around me. These people were living as content a life as could be expected under the grim circumstances; they had created a sanctuary, a commune of hope. It was then I realized that no one inside here was wearing a bracelet. Or if they were, the units weren't activated. The residents of the zoo were off the grid.

"How did it get this way?" I asked Zac. "What happened to the zoo?"

"I remember there being financial troubles," he said, gathering the details in his head, "after a gang broke in and let a lot of the animals loose. It was pretty ugly. Some of the gangers were mangled, and one of them died from being bit in the face by a monkey. Then, a few months after the zoo recovered from that, someone snuck in and poisoned a lot of the animals. Then the plague. So, without any paying customers or donations, it closed down and moved to a wildlife preserve built outside the city, north of Sausalito, which sparked a minor uprising—you know, animals being allowed to leave the quarantine but not humans."

"That hole we crawled through, that came from the gangers?"

"I'm not sure. My father showed it to me."

"Your father?"

"He used it when he broke in to put up the graffiti."

"Your father is responsible for these messages here and around the city?"

"Yes, he is," Zac stated proudly. "I don't know about all the ones around the city. There have been a lot of copycats, I think. But definitely the ones here. Come on, I'll show you some more."

On the side of the Leaping Lemur Café was one I had seen before:

HOPE IS THE FALLOUT

OF DESPAIR

And scrawled upon a four-by-eight-foot piece of plywood leaning against a research building was another:

IF REBIRTH ADMITS DEFEAT,

THEN DEATH TRIUMPHS

On the domed roof of the nearby carousel, visible in the sudden, glaring illumination of a motion-activated safety light, was:

BE OUR FUTURE'S PAST,

NOT ITS END

Unfortunately, Zac and I were also well lit.

We heard a murmur of indiscernible voices tumble from the dark. Without a word, Zac bolted! He was several strides gone before I, too, ran, mimicking his zigzag route through a playground and a line of trees to a long stretch of paved pathway. I had tried to prepare for this assignment in as many ways as I could, but getting in shape was not one of them. My legs cramped; my heart and lungs neared eruption. Zac ran and ran, never looking back to see if I was with him. My feeble attempts to shout for him to slow down were lost in asthmatic gasps for air.

We rounded a turn and approached a white building— an aviary, I thought it was—and looming over me as I passed one of its tall walls was:

GOD

HATES

COWARDS

I took my eyes from those haunting words to discover I had lost Zac. He was not on the path in front of me or anywhere to be seen.

I slowed to a stiff hobble. Concerned I would rouse the tent dwellers, I tried to stifle my labored breaths, which only brought on a fit of deep, painful coughs. I bent forward to spit out crud from my lungs and then straightened, too quickly, and became dizzy and teetering. As I regained equilibrium, I recognized my surroundings as the spot where we had come in. There was a hand on my shoulder, and I spun, almost falling over.

"What are you doing? We have to get out of here," Zac said, frustrated and desperate. He skulked away into the grouping of trees through which we had arrived.

Just before hunkering into the secret hole once more, I paused in the damp grass to see our pursuers. Yet, there were no voices in the dark or footsteps upon the pathway, not a glimpse of anyone. Intentionally or not, I felt duped. And I wasn't happy about it. Also, I didn't like sneaking around, spying like a voyeuristic tabloid reporter. I was there to observe and learn, and I wasn't going to do that lurking in the shadows. By the time I crawled out the other side, I had made a decision.

Zac was already across the boulevard, waving for me to join him. Instead, I walked back the way we'd come, toward the zoo's entrance.

I could hear Zac's panicked voice. "What...Where are you going? Get over here!"

I continued walking. Not surprising, it took considerably less time to cover the distance that we had previously crawled. I reached the corner of the parking lot, and rather than heading right, toward the neighborhood, I turned left and made my way to the zoo's main entrance. As I walked, I brushed off the dirt and grime I had acquired from our little adventure.

It was only moments later that I heard Zac coming up

behind me, his breathing rapid and tense. "Mr. Garrett. Mr. Garrett?" he gasped.

"You don't have to come with me if you don't want to," I told him.

About a hundred feet ahead of us, two grizzly-size men walked our way and then stopped, allowing us to approach. Behind them were three more men of similar build. A reinforced fence of scrap wood and old tires lined the walkway on either side of a gate constructed of welded junk iron that was the community's entranceway. One of the men, all obviously guards, put a hand up for us to halt.

"We're going to ask you to turn around and leave the way you came," he said.

"Please, excuse this intrusion," I began. "My name is Aaron Garrett. I'm with the *Sound*, an online news source, and I'm here in the city to write about life here after all that has happened." I removed the stack of paperwork and credentials from my jacket and handed them over to the guard who'd spoken to us, as he seemed to be the one in charge. "I'm staying with my friend here, a few blocks away, and he told me about your community. I'm very interested in learning more, if any of you might grant me an interview."

Zac anxiously paced next to me, dampening my credibility. At one point, the second guard motioned for him to step back. I looked down and noticed a broad yellow line, part of a semicircle that stretched outward from about fifty feet on either side of the gate into the parking lot. A boundary, which Zac had stepped over, that an outsider could not cross.

"Odd time to be out reporting," the guard said as he returned my papers.

"True," I replied. "I want to see the city from every angle, at all hours."

It was then, as though on cue, that I became aware of a distant pulse of music and the noise of a crowd, laughing, hollering, and screaming. It was difficult to tell from which direction it came. "Apparently life goes on here, curfew or not," I added.

"That's the parade," Zac stated.

After a moment of thought, the guard said, "It's too late right now. Come back at nine a.m., and we'll see."

"What was your name?" I asked him.

"Gabe."

"Well, thank you, Gabe. I apologize again for this late intrusion. I will see you at nine." As I began to offer him my hand to shake on our agreement, Zac stopped me and moved us away.

"It's discourteous to offer them any physical contact," Zac whispered as we left the five men.

"Did you notice that none of them are wearing bracelets?" I asked him.

"Of course. That's why I asked you to cover yours up when we were inside."

"How did they all avoid getting tagged?"

"I don't know." Zac shrugged dismissively. "They're homeless. They don't matter, I guess."

A few steps farther, Gabe called out to us, "Be careful of the parade."

*   *   *

It had been known by different names: the Halloween Procession, the All-Saints Parade, the March of the Dead, the Gruesome Gala, and most common, simply the parade. But no matter what it was called, everyone understood it as a macabre Mardi Gras that snaked its way through every neighborhood, along every street in the city, for weeks from the first day of fall, embracing and celebrating the death and misery that has become such an integral part of life there.

Initially, of course, the authorities shut down the festivities—it violated curfew and crossed into clean and unclean zones. But their attempts were futile, as the march would simply manifest itself within another neighborhood, and further hindrance by the military or the police incited violence. So compromises were made—as with other prior circumstances—"in an effort to prevent a situation of unrest."

Thus, the gala was allowed to proceed as long as it was policed and zones were not mixed. From this, then, came two separate marches: one in the secured, "clean" parts of the city and the other contained within the unsecured, "contaminated" areas. This inspired yet another descriptive of the event: the Festival of Life and Dark.

(When I questioned someone as to why it wasn't "Life

and *Death*," the response was, "Because being infected isn't always a death sentence. Some people survive[†] and are moved into the secure zone, into the side of light and living." When I queried as to why, then, it wasn't "*Light* and Dark," I received a blank stare.)

I was told more than once that the "dark" procession was more interesting, as well as more grisly, to witness. Also, at some point, the course of the two parades would converge, arriving simultaneously to a street designated as a boundary between zones with spectacular and tenuous results. This became considerably more arranged than fortuitous. Van Ness Avenue was the most common sight of the occurrence. Knowing that, the police converged there as well.

As Zac and I made our way home from the zoo, I asked him if we could take a look at the parade I could tell wasn't far off.

"That's not a good idea," he told me. "Spectators aren't really allowed."

"How can they stop people from watching?" I said.

"Well, nothing can be done about people looking out their windows or watching from rooftops. But if they can, they'll grab you and make you march. The police patrol the perimeter and arrest anyone who gets too close."

"On what grounds?"

"The same way a person can be arrested for attempting suicide. It's for their own protection. Or if it's past curfew, of

---

[†] There were only two on record.

course."

"But it's okay to be out past curfew if you're marching."

"Yep."

"And spectators are forced to march?"

"They say it's like life. You can't be a spectator and really be alive. You have to experience it. They say you have to participate."

"'Surviving is not living.'"

"Yep."

"Who are 'they'?"

"Who are who?"

"Who started this whole thing? Who organizes it?" I clarified.

"I don't know," replied Zac. "It just sort of happens."

I doubted that was true; someone or some group had to be organizing the event. Instead of pressing the matter, I stopped and listened. I could hear the parade calling out to me to join it—not in a seductive whisper, either, but with a growl, like a challenge. My grandfather once told me that when he was very young, the holiday of Halloween lasted only a single night. But a lot has changed since then, with the third world war and the plague, with riots dividing cities and the country, and with violence from Cross Hunters leaving churches and temples in ashes and ministers hung or shot, or worse. (I would find out from Ben that his father's church was torched twice, and he had to take his ministry underground.) Here the holiday lasts days upon weeks, having grown longer each year. Considering recent history, it all seemed normal, even natural.

I considered the household in which I was staying. While there was evidence of normalcy in place—watching television, enjoying a good book, meeting around the table for dinner after a long day—its behavior was distinctly artificial, its happiness forced, like the shelf of carefully selected photographs. Of course, I understood their longing for comfort and security, and how maintaining daily routines was a mechanism by which to cope, but I couldn't deny how unnatural it felt, as though it might have been healthier to relinquish complacency and relish anger, sorrow, and gloom. It felt right to shout and cry—and march. It was certainly what I wanted to do as I reflected upon my first day there. As I fell asleep, once again, upon my saggy cot, I forgot about my assignment and what I was there to do. I wanted to do more than observe and ask questions. I didn't want to be a spectator. I wanted to be a part of what was happening, to participate.

FUTURE'S PAST

When I was ten years old, I accompanied my father to the Washington State Convention and Trade Center, a beautiful structure of glass and steel spanning two city blocks in downtown Seattle. Being a teacher, he was to attend a conference on education; I went with him the day before as he picked up a name tag and a packet outlining the seminars for which he had enrolled. I remember riding the escalators and running around the lush urban garden outside the top floor. At lunch, we sat in an area that had a conceptual art installation on display made up of lighted signs that flashed and scrolled different messages—"truisms," as they were called—from the late twentieth-century work of artist Jenny Holzer.

Intrigued and mesmerized, I insisted on writing them down. My father gave me a pen and a sheet of paper from his packet (a summary of a lecture on "conformity in the classroom"), and I frantically scribbled on the back of it as words sped by. I wrote down over a dozen before my father said it was time to go. That night at home, I copied them into a notebook, which would become my first journal. It was Holzer's concept of language as art that inspired me to be a writer.

As I lay on my uncomfortable cot, woken by Zac's snoring and Ben's restless tossing, I thought about Samuel Elliot's own messages and how they reminded me of those truisms from my childhood. I couldn't help but imagine Samuel Elliot at the convention center with my father and me that day, watching that same art installation. Was he inspired as well? Did he have an interest in contemporary education, or was he just getting out of the rain? Was he sitting next to us at lunch? If so, what kind of sandwich did he eat? Or perhaps he was alone, brooding in a corner. Was he even the brooding type?

It wasn't quite seven a.m. when I limped down the hall, stiff and sore from my unsupportive sleeping surface and the previous night's activities. I carried my Moleskine so that I could review my notes from the day before, part of my morning ritual. Mrs. Elliot sat at the dining table with a cup of tea.

"Would you like some breakfast?" Mrs. Elliot asked me. "We have cereal, eggs, bread, and bagels. We went through our ration of breakfast meat already, though. We have juice, tea, and coffee, too, if you like."

"Some toast and juice would be great, thank you."

Nikki was in her spot on the couch; she gave me a "good

morning" glance and resumed reading, doing exactly what she would be doing the rest of the day.

"Can I ask what you're reading?"

"P. W. Gohr, *By a Dark Stream*," she answered without looking up from her screen.

I knew the book; I had read the original paper version. I recalled the likeness of a soaring raven on its cover. It was the allegorical tale of a soldier living in a time of peace who ventured away from his village time and again to deliberately face the beasts and terrors of the forest. It was the only way he felt alive.

Mrs. Elliot returned with my breakfast.

"I have an appointment at nine this morning to visit the zoo community," I mentioned. I began to explain how Zac and I had been there but thought it best not to get him involved. Instead, I told her that I had arranged the meeting prior to my arrival.

Mrs. Elliot nodded and went back to the kitchen, saying, "Peter and Jacqueline will be joining us soon. I need to get them something to eat."

"She's not stupid," Nikki whispered to me from across the room. "She knows all about Zac's adventures after curfew."

"Noted," I told her. Then I asked, "Have you read a lot of Gohr?"

"Most of it," she replied.

"That one's not the best for escapism, is it? It's not one

of his lighter ones, I mean. "

"I'm not trying to escape. I find General Barthram[†] interesting. I like his ideals. Facing horrors rather than hiding from them."

"You don't think it desensitized him?"

"No, I actually think it made him more empathetic, which is his downfall. He cared too much."

"Is that possible?"

"If you lose yourself in the process," interjected Mrs. Elliot from the kitchen, "then what good are you to anyone?"

Peter and his mother came from their room and joined me at the table. I wished them a good morning. He returned the courtesy, and his mother sat, gazing nervously from her twitching fingers upon the table to the silent television set behind her. I found her pained demeanor difficult to watch. Peter gently placed a hand over hers and said, "Let's have something to eat first." Probably the same thing he said to her every morning.

I agreed with Peter, while his mother was a story, one that represented many in the city, she was not the story I was looking for. I never found out what had happened that would leave her in such a state of nearly catatonic shock. What I did know was that she was a small part of a collective tragedy. We all were.

In the Elliot home, however, Jacqueline Miller was cared for; they aided her in her healing. I couldn't imagine

---

[†] Gohr's wayward soldier.

her condition being any worse, yet the others admitted she was getting better, and it wouldn't be long before Peter would move her out of the city (all part of his carefully laid plan).

Mrs. Elliot returned with two plates of scrambled eggs and toast. Peter and his mother ate, and I continued my conversation with Nikki.

"Did you lose your family to the plague?" I asked her.

Nikki stopped reading and looked directly at me. From her, it was a little disconcerting. "I was separated from my mother and my sister during one of the riots. They got out of the city and I didn't." She spoke as though reciting a prepared statement. "They avoided arrest in Sacramento behind the defense of their civil liberties being violated. The lawyers couldn't help me, though. Now I wait. When I make it another five months, I'll be able to join them."

"What happened to your father?" I asked.

"He's dead."

She went back to her book; our conversation was done.

Peter leaned close to me and said, "You might remember Nikki in the news about ten years ago."

I thought a moment, and I did recall a Nikki Chin who, at the age of nine, became infamous for pushing her father into the path of a speeding BART train for one too many abusive nights. I also remembered how the media—true to its fashion of exploiting the sensational and subverting the heart—had put an inappropriate amount of attention on the morbid details of her abuse and Mr. Chin's gory demise. Little regard was given to the heroic girl who refused to be a victim.

Once an individual was tested and found neither to be infected nor a carrier, they would be moved to a clean zone and periodically retested. If after eighteen months they remained negative, that individual would be allowed to leave the city. I understood, then, Nikki's apprehension to being out of doors; she didn't want to take too many chances. (She didn't want to hide away from horrors, either, like the soldier, Barthram.) So Nikki sat, patiently reading and waiting—still refusing to be a victim—and holding fast to the day she would be reunited with her mother and sister and get on with her life.

Ben entered the room, and it was like turning on a light. Sullen Nikki offered him a smile; Mrs. Elliot beamed and asked him what he would like for breakfast.

"French toast!" he answered.

She gave him a look that lovingly said he was going to get whatever she gave him and like it. With a shrug, he said, "I know, it's not Sunday. I'll have cereal."

Mrs. Elliot went to the kitchen once again. I took another look at the corner of photographs. There was one in a bright-red lacquered frame: a portrait of a middle-aged woman with a distinctly American appearance and a young girl who looked to be Nikki's twin. On a lower shelf sat a portrait of Ben appearing uncharacteristically humorless.

Another picture had Zac in the kitchen, putting together what appeared to be a rather complicated meal, and next to it was a snapshot I found particularly interesting: Dane and Zac, arms around each other, smiling as though having shared an intimate joke or a kiss.

Before I could comment, Nikki was off the couch and standing beside me, pointing at Ben's morose portrait. "That's my favorite," she said.

"What do you think has him so dour?" I asked with a grin.

"He must have been writing in his journal," Nikki replied. "It's the only time I see him look like that."

"So you're a writer," I said to Ben.

As I mentioned, I've read his blog. But it was shut down when martial law was enacted. "For security reasons" was the official statement. But to curb any negative publicity (as though martial law wasn't negative enough) that might instill more rioting was the largest part of it. I was intrigued that Ben continued to chronicle his life and the events around him. *He must have something to say*, I thought to myself.

"I just keep a journal," he muttered with a shrug.

"He's got volumes," Nikki added.

"Many great writers keep a journal. And not-so-great writers, too, like me," I told him.

"I've read some of his essays for school," said Peter. "He's good."

"He takes after his father like that, with his writing,"

Mrs. Elliot added as she brought Ben his bowl of cereal and milk. "Samuel enjoyed words."

"I'd like to see some of your husband's writing, if I could," I said.

"He wasn't so much a writer as a speaker."

"You can say that again," Ben commented with a chuckle.

"He did like to talk, didn't he, sweetie?" Mrs. Elliot replied.

Peter and Nikki sighed in agreement.

"He liked to sermonize, did he?" I said.

"You could say that."

"He would ramble," Ben explained, "like he was always thinking out loud."

"What was his background, religiously?" I asked Mrs. Elliot.

"He grew up Presbyterian," she answered. "But his own ministry had no particular denomination."

"Universal Life?"

"No. Samuel didn't believe in any religion, only God."

"But he had a church," I said.

"Only as a place for people to get together."

Religion was not a part of my childhood, yet neither were my parents atheists. I never actually knew what their beliefs were, and the presence of a supreme divinity was not something I'd ever felt. Spiritual ambivalence was the foundation of my impious life. However, I knew enough to understand that Samuel Elliot's convictions were unconventional.

"I want to state," Mrs. Elliot said, pausing to be sure she had my attention, "that my husband was not responsible for the Omega virus. Neither its creation nor its release."

She then waited to see that I wrote down her statement.

"You've been speaking of your husband in the past tense," I said. "Is he...no longer with us?"

"We can't say for sure," admitted Mrs. Elliot, looking away. "I fear for the worst. Besides, if I do know his whereabouts, I won't say until his name is cleared."

Ben stood from the table—quite suddenly, it seemed—and took his empty cereal bowl to the kitchen. Mrs. Elliot went silent as I looked for a distraction from the clumsy moment.

I found it in the red framed photograph I saw earlier and said to Nikki, "Your mother and sister?"

"Yes. They sent that one to me recently." She lingered on that and then said, "I'm so glad that they got the hell out of here."

"Can I ask what happened? How did you get separated from them?"

"Ever been in a riot?"

"No," I told her. "Can you tell me about it?"

"We were returning from an extended trip to Hawaii," she said. "It [the release of the virus] happened while we were gone. We didn't even live in San Francisco; we lived down south in San Mateo. If our plane had been just fifteen minutes later on its approach, the three of us would have been diverted to Sacramento, and we would still be together."

"But your plane landed."

"A lot of passengers had already deplaned when the panic started, all because some idiot was screaming about how the airport was to be closed down from the quarantine. Well, everyone freaked, of course. People rushed to board the plane while half of us were still on it. I pushed my sister and mother back into their seats and told them to buckle up. I thought it would be safer than being caught in the aisle. It turned out I was right, because I was knocked down and dragged from the plane as others forced themselves on board.

"Flight attendants fought to close the door, and the pilot taxied the plane away from the terminal until things calmed down. Then it was decided they would fly off to Sacramento, and well, I wasn't on the plane. The violence escalated. I was lucky to get out of there with nothing but a cut lip and sprained shoulder. I called Zac and he picked me up in Millbrae and brought me here. The next day, the airport was shut down and the city quarantined."

"And here you've been," said Mrs. Elliot. She crossed the room and put her arms around Nikki. "Just five more months, dear."

"I know."

I asked Mrs. Elliot, "How much longer do you have to stay?"

"We don't intend to leave," she replied. "This is our home."

"Where would we go, anyway?" Dane said as she entered the room. She wore the T-shirt and shorts she most likely had slept in and went into the kitchen to get her own breakfast. I watched her collect her coffee, bagel, and glass of juice. Her torso was longer than her legs, and she had a figure more like an adolescent boy developing muscles than a woman in her early twenties. She was rough, but the night's sleep had softened her edge. There was an alluring melancholy about her; I began to appreciate Ben's infatuation with her. The dichotomy of her wildness and gloom was arresting. It only took a glance from her to draw you in, and her gently curled, sad grin was the hook.

"Wouldn't anywhere be better than here?" I asked Dane. She sat across from me at the table.

"One place is as sick as another out there," she replied. "Sometimes euthanizing the whole damn planet *does* sound like a pretty good idea."

"Dane!" snapped Mrs. Elliot. Her pleasant demeanor was so suddenly replaced by admonition and contempt that it asphyxiated the room into silence.

I still had another hour before my appointment at the zoo, so I decided it was time to go through my notes. As I thumbed through the pages of my Moleskine notebook, Dane looked over at my open page and, after finishing a mouthful of bagel, said, "It's green."

"What's green?"

"The notes you're writing there."

I looked down at the graphite-gray text I had written with a mechanical pencil and smiled. "How long have you had your condition?"

"For as long as I can remember. At first, I thought everybody could see the colors of sounds and words. But I got a lot of weird looks when I talked about it."

"All sounds?"

"No. For me, it's usually sharp or sustained tones of a particular pitch," she said. Looking over to the television, she continued. "Like the game show they're watching. There's a buzzer that goes off when a contestant gets an answer wrong."

We both watched and waited.

BZZZZ!

I turned to her.

"Purple and lime-green shards of glass," she said, "sort of snowing in my peripheral vision." There went another *BZZZZ!* and she smiled.

I made a note about her condition as Mrs. Elliot, still tense, reminded me I had an appointment to keep.

"Where are you going?" Dane asked me.

"I'm hoping to talk to some of the people living in the zoo," I told her.

"Mind if I come along?"

"Of course not."

*   *   *

I had wanted to go to the zoo by myself. I didn't want to jeopardize the trust I had earned with Gabe, the guard. He was my key to getting inside. However, something told me I could depend on Dane not to hinder my efforts.

The two of us followed the same route to the zoo's entrance as Zac and I had the night before. Of course, the atmosphere was different. The sky was clear, an invigorating wind blew, a few children played in the street; it felt like a Sunday instead of a weekday. Traffic was minimal to nonexistent. We walked down the middle of the street instead of the sidewalk because, well, we could.

"How did you find out about zoo-town?" Dane asked me.

"Zac showed—told me about it."

"Took you through his little hole, did he? Someone should plug that thing up, leave those people in peace; although, I have considered moving in there myself a few times." She gave me a grin and a wink.

We passed that one burned-out building, which looked less threatening in the sunlight; the fire that brought it down must have burned for some time, as there was little left but a mound of charcoal and mud framed within the structure's crumbled foundation. Weeds and ground cover gave life to its muted colors, lightened its graven shape. I noticed how the two buildings beside the remains were charred but relatively intact, as though the fire had been allowed to burn but not spread. Dane stopped to look at it; she gazed upon it a little longer than seemed warranted.

"Zac said it used to be some kind of community center, right?" I confirmed.

Tight-lipped, she nodded and moved on.

The expanse of the lush, forested "zoo-town" waited for us across the wide boulevard—again, with only a little more traffic than there had been at midnight. Along the shore to our right, a soothing layer of ocean mist spread beneath the blue sky.

Dane sighed. "It's a shame this had to happen to such a beautiful city. It figures that I had to decide to live here, of all the places in the world I could have picked." Dane left home—Puerto Rico—at the age of fourteen. She lived in a number of US cities over the course of a year before ending up in the Bay Area. "I connected with this city in that it was nearly surrounded by water, like an island," she explained, "and neighborhoods like the Mission reminded me of home. It was comforting. I needed that. But it was new, too, and so beautiful."

After a couple of years growing up on its streets, she took the city's name as her own. Though she had grown up in her mother's house in San Germán and knew of her father, Dane Francisco considered herself an orphan, "the casualty of a Puerto Rican woman and a Haitian man's drunken copulation."

Dane's gaze was taken by the greens and browns of the zoo's forest, and she said, "We used to make calls here. We would run tests on them regularly, at least once a week, to make sure they stayed uninfected. They were always healthy; we never had to release anyone inside there."

"How did they get away with not wearing these bracelets?"

"I don't know. I always thought of it as another example of our government's incompetence."

"You don't go in there anymore?" I asked.

"No. They've prohibited outsiders ever since a band of reapers pretending to be us got to them. Instead of drawing blood for a test, they injected almost a dozen of them with an undiluted version of the same thing we use, a dose to kill instantly."

"Reapers?"

"Months ago, a few attendants went rogue. They decided that what we do should go beyond those infected with the Omega. The homeless, the elderly, the handicapped, whomever they deem to be without hope or purpose. And they've grown in numbers, with followers and copycats."

"So, what, they run around randomly euthanizing people?"

"Yes."

"They got to a dozen in there," I thought out loud.

"Almost." Her voice faded, and she hung back a few

paces as we drew closer to the entrance.

There was a man waiting, but it wasn't Gabe. He was small and thin, elderly, and he stood within the designated safe area, the yellow semicircle that curved out across the sidewalk and into the parking lot. (Could it really have been that simple to avoid viral contamination?) He waited, steely and immovable. Flanking him were two large, impressively goonish men. I hadn't noticed the night before, but now in the morning light, it was easy to see painted on the junk-constructed entrance gate the words:

FUTURE'S

PAST

"Are you Mr. Garrett?" the man asked as I stopped just outside the circle. He may have been elderly, but there was nothing frail about him. Intimidation seemed natural for him, in his posture, his glare, and his humorless voice.

"Yes. I was supposed to meet Gabe," I replied.

"Gabe is indisposed. I understand that you are here to investigate us."

"I wouldn't say that, no. I'm in the city for a couple of days to write about life inside the quarantine. It's purely objective."

"How did you find out about us?"

"Someone I'm staying with told me. What was your name again?"

"We're very private people, Mr. Garrett. I've met you here to tell you that we don't want to be written about, and we don't allow outsiders into our community, especially after last night."

"What happened last night?"

"We had uninvited guests. They came in through a hole we discovered."

"You should have everyone tested," said Dane, taking a step forward.

The man turned his stoic glare upon her and asked, "And who are you, young lady? You look familiar." He looked at her bright-green bracelet. Like the residents I had seen the night before, he was without one.

"My name is Dane Francisco. I'm an attendant with the FCO. I used to do examinations here."

"I remember. Yes. Thank you for your concern, but we can do our own health assessments."

The entrance gates began to part, painfully creaking open like the mouth of an ancient beast. Just inside, a group had gathered; whether reinforcements or curious onlookers, I couldn't tell, but they watched Dane and me intensely. One man stood out from the rest. He was over a foot taller than everyone else. A long, thin beard lengthened his narrow face, and the thick lenses of his glasses greatly magnified his eyes. *A bearded praying mantis peering through the underbrush,* I thought to myself. Once the elderly man and his goons were inside, the gates immediately began to churn closed behind them. I took a step to follow, but Dane grabbed my sleeve.

"Well, that was weird," I mumbled as the gates shut

with a blunt finality. I stopped a moment. I felt a little bitter; I took the rejection personally. An ocean gust threw sand at my shoes.

"You've seen those messages, right?" I then said to Dane, pointing to the words in front of us. "Zac told me his father put them up."

We started our walk back to the house. "Yes, I've seen them," she responded with a resonance of regretful disappointment.

"They seem to have had an impact on people—I mean, to be copied around town," I commented.

"Desperate people, maybe," she snapped. "They're just fortune cookies, you know. They're only worth what people make of them. And idiots grasping at reality make the most out of them."

"True. But I can't help but be intrigued," I told her, "because I am a reality-grasping idiot. What can you tell me about Samuel Elliot?"

"What do want to know about him?" she asked, resigning with a sigh.

"I want to know something about the man behind those messages, ridiculous or not."

"He was a minister with a following that trusted him," Dane said.

"Were you one of them?"

"Not at first. At first, he was just Zac's dad. As a minister, he had a way of making the idea of God reasonable and rational—you know, believable. And I had no reason to believe anything before I met him. But do I know of anything he said to indicate why he would spray-paint a zoo or set off a virus to kill millions of people?" She answered her own question with a shrug.

"So you don't think he could've done it."

"The messages? Sure. He used to say things like that in his sermons, little prophetic sound bites. And if Zac says he painted them, then I've got no reason not to believe him."

There was a lull, the sound of our feet upon asphalt filling the silence between us.

"Mrs. Elliot swears Samuel had nothing to do with the Omega," I said. "What do you think?"

With a contemptuous tone, she said, "I hope not."

Samuel Elliot's influence was evident in the preservation of his messages on the zoo grounds and their reproduction in places throughout the city. *Who were his followers, and how many were there? I wondered. One zealous lunatic desperate for a purpose or hundreds of individuals searching for guidance? Were Samuel's esoteric words that shining light?*

"What do you believe, Dane?" I asked her again as we started down the street to the house.

"About what?"

"Samuel Elliot. Average neighborhood minister? Prophet? Goofy, misunderstood, demented cultist?"

She mulled the question over and stopped at the front

steps of the house, looking up to be sure no one was within earshot. "He was like a father to me," she said, "and yes, I think he could have done it. I think he had it in him to do it, anyway. Did Zac tell you why his father snuck into the zoo?"

"To spray graffiti, I thought."

"No, that was an afterthought. He broke in to poison the animals, to put them out of their sad, miserable existence, as he saw it. So I wouldn't put it past him to have done the same thing on a much larger scale."

"A massive mercy killing?"

With a resolute shake of her head, Dane turned and started up the steps. "I believe he could have done it."

*   *   *

Zac was finally up and halfway through a feta-and-spinach omelet he had made for himself when we returned to the house. He asked where we had been, and I reminded him of my meeting at the zoo.

"Oh, that's right," he said. "How did it go?"

"There's something odd going on there. Something they don't want anyone to know about," I told him.

"I told you they're pretty leery of strangers."

With Zac having breakfast and Ben occupied with schoolwork, I went back to their room, where I could have a moment of privacy to rethink the morning. However, within minutes, Zac had finished eating and joined me in the cramped bedroom. It was obvious he had a question or wanted to somehow be involved in whatever I was doing; it seemed our outing the night before had been a bonding experience for him. However, I felt otherwise.

"I wanted to show you something—I mean, play something for you," he said.

"Okay. What is it?"

He checked the hall before closing the door. Moving aside a stack of magazines next to the shortwave radio, he removed what looked like a cassette tape. (I can't say that I had ever seen one before.) It was all very secretive. He inserted the tape into a unit that was part of the radio.

"I've had this old shortwave a long time," he explained. "I don't know, there's a kind of magic in the way it picks up stuff from the other side of the planet. It makes the world seem far away, not in a computer or right outside the door." He pressed the play button and added, "I recorded this a couple months ago. It's broadcast out of South America, I think."

As I had mentioned, I once had a similar radio. I never enjoyed using it, however, because I found it difficult to listen to; the shortwave method of broadcast was appropriately named, as the signal always seemed to be riding a "wave" in the way it would fade in and out—one moment clear, the next broken and indiscernible. Tuning in to hear news or music "from the other side of the planet" often became an exercise in frustration for me.

Zac's recording was no different. I could tell it was the voice of a man, just talking, and I could make out a few words or a sentence, but then it would fade to static, as though someone were turning the volume up and down in a slow, regular rhythm. Loud and clear, then gone. Clarity and static. Now you hear it; now you don't.

I listened carefully. I was able to make out "...sermon, it should be lived..." and then "...at our fingertips..." followed by "...then death triumphs..."

"It's hard to understand, Zac. What is this?"

"I'm pretty sure it's my father," he said. "I know it's not a very good recording, but I'm pretty sure it's him."

I strained again to hear.

"...construct by men within...sacred texts inside...smoldering embers...God was not..."

Ben came into the room, and both Zac and I jumped. "I'm sorry, I didn't know you—" he began, then stopped at the sight of the two of us and the tape player. He quickly closed the door, saying, "What are you doing? Mom might hear!"

"Where is she?" Zac asked him.

"Talking to Peter."

"Well, keep an ear out for her."

"Your mother doesn't want you hearing this?" I said.

"She doesn't know we have it. I don't want her to hear it," Ben said firmly.

"She might want to hear it, knowing that it's him," Zac said.

"You don't know that it's him," said Ben with an ear to

the door. "You can barely understand it."

The recording finished, all ninety seconds of it. (I came to know how long it was because of how many times I would listen to it.) I asked Ben, "So you don't think it's your father?"

"It can't be him," Ben replied.

"You know it could," Zac shot back. "It's one of his sermons. I recognize it."

"No, you don't," said Ben. "It only sounds like one. He didn't go to South America."

"How do you know?" I had to ask.

"I just know" was Ben's reserved answer.

Wanting to hear the broadcast again, I asked Zac if he had a pair of earphones. The two of them, awed by my apparent stroke of genius, rummaged through the debris of their room until Zac found a set, its wires twisted and kinked. They worked, though, and I listened three more times to the fragmented broadcast that began "...the written word...visceral..." and ended with "...my belief became..."

I began to appreciate, after all, the "bonding" Zac and I had gone through. The recording was important; whether or not the voice belonged to Samuel Elliot didn't matter as much to me as the fact that Zac believed so strongly that it was his father and that Ben was so confident that it wasn't. To understand why, I needed to discern as much of the broadcast as possible. The brothers watched me intently as I played and rewound and played and rewound the tape; they seemed to be waiting for some sort of verdict as to who was right, which, of course, was impossible for me to say. It was also impossible for me to concentrate with them hovering.

"Maybe you should step out and keep your mother distracted," I told them.

The brothers left me with my notebook in front of me on the floor and earphones plugged into the player. Then I glanced to my right and saw them—a substantial pile of composition books underneath Ben's bed, the same kind of books I used to use to write *my* journal.

(As I said, my intention when Zac and Ben left the room was to sit with that alleged recording of their father and decipher as much of it as I could. I just wanted to clarify that, for I'm not proud of what I *did* do, which was in no way premeditated.)

I reached out and took one of those composition books, as casually as if I were in my own room at the age of thirteen and it was my own notebook beneath my own bed. It didn't matter that the handwriting wasn't mine (Ben's was actually legible) and that none of the books or entries were dated (as I would have done), but instead were snippets of random thoughts. Not empty thoughts. Rather, observations with insights I would expect from the young man with whom I sat on the shore. I began to read them in much the same spirit as they were written, by randomly grabbing books from the pile and aimlessly choosing sections, like the following:

Peter and Zac have known each other for as long as I can remember. I hardly know him, though, and he's been living here for over a month. Now he wants to move his mother in with us, too. I haven't met her. Mom said he was a saint, and Nik said he was so nice he wasn't real. I remember people making fun of him in school, like he was slow, but he was just quiet and kept to himself, I think. I will say that he always did seem to know what was going on, before everyone else.

— — —

Zac told me about a news report he just heard, broadcast all the way from Africa! He said a group of people were captured and arrested in the Congo for killing three other people for poaching. Zac thinks they are some of Dad's radical friends and wondered if Dad was with them. I told them they were never friends, and of course, he wasn't in Africa.

— — —

I wish I knew what I'm supposed to do. Everyone else seems to have a place to go or a job to do. Sometimes I feel like I'm taking up space. Dad used to tell me I was the future and that it was a responsibility no one else envied. I guess that's something.

— — —

We met Dane's new partner, Quigley. [Ben must've written this one just that morning.] *She said she knew him from before, when he worked in the crematorium, and she wanted to work with him because his voice had color. She meant that when he spoke, or something about a noise he made that effected her (or is it affected? I can never remember the difference). I teased her that maybe it was more than his voice that e/affected her.*

— — —

I hate eggs and Zac always insists on making everyone omelets on Sunday mornings. What's wrong with pancakes? Everyone likes pancakes, too. Then again, I like French toast and that has eggs in it. Man, I'd wish he'd turn off that stupid radio! The buses are going to start running again tomorrow. It'll be nice to get out of the neighborhood.

— — —

Dane's having a bad night. I have to remind myself she's not perfect. She's not open, and she can be obstinate, having to have things her way. In school, I remember, she always seemed to be looking for a fight. But then, why shouldn't she be that way, growing up on the streets? She put herself through high school while working at a veterinary clinic. I think she even lived there for a while, sleeping on a couch in an office upstairs and bathing in the sink normally used for washing dogs. She made her own way. I used to be jealous of Zac—or any guy she looks at in a way that I wish she would look at me.

One passage in particular grabbed my attention. It was part of a much longer entry, one that went on for several pages. It read:

"*Then, vulnerable and weakened by the pandemic, the survivors would find solace and strength in creating a new world order built on communal, worldwide peace, selflessness, and newfound reverence for the lives and needs of others. The good news for the damned is the bond of hope it creates. That would be my second wish."*

He closed his eyes and looked upward as though he were wishing for all that right then and there. Zac and I looked around to see if it might come true.

Then I asked—

My snooping was interrupted by a voice I hadn't heard in that house before. As I entered the hall, Dane was coming out of her room ahead of me at a deliberate pace. She went into the living room, where Zac and a guy built like a plank of wood—skinny, with wide shoulders, a flat chest and stomach, and no chin—stood talking. Dane didn't say anything but planted herself like a sentry waiting for the slightest provocation. Ben hovered nearby, and there was a strange, stoic character with long greasy hair and a grossly prominent chin waiting by the front door.

It was Peter, having abruptly emerged from his room, who expressed what Dane appeared to be thinking. "What are you doing here?" he asked. His tone was sharp and staccato, and he placed himself between his mother and this new character, who gave me a wary look.

"Who the hell are you?" he asked me.

Peter answered, "This is Aaron Garrett, a writer out of Seattle. Aaron, this is Drake, my stepbrother."

Drake wasn't surprised or put off by the welcome he'd

received. He feigned a caring glance to Jacqueline, his stepmother, then gave a condescending sneer to Peter. Though Drake stood a foot taller, I would've guessed that Peter had at least twenty pounds on him. Unlike his companion at the door, Drake's long black hair was clean and groomed, complementing his well-chosen attire of a leather jacket, silk shirt, tight jeans, and snakeskin boots. Drake was the type who put effort into being the center of attention, as he was at that moment.

"He just stopped by to ask for my help with something," Zac interjected.

Drake looked around the room as though somehow vindicated. Then he shook my hand with a grip that attempted to impress me, which it didn't. "I'd sure like to talk to you about life outside of here," he said. "Maybe I'll see you later." Before leaving, he confirmed some plans with Zac. "So you can do it?"

Zac twisted his mouth in thought before replying. "She can't get a ride from someone at work?"

"I don't trust any of those gumps she works with. And you can't expect her to walk to the bus. It's five blocks away."

"No, of course not," Zac mumbled.

"I usually pick her up whenever she works, but I just can't tonight."

"Sure, I'll do it," Zac finally said.

"That's 'dise, Zac. Thanks." Drake dropped a set of keys into Zac's hand. "I've got tonight's location programmed into the system, so you shouldn't have any trouble finding it. She should finish up work around midnight. I don't have to tell you to be careful."

"I'll drive her like she were my own."

"No. You'll drive it like it's *mine*."

As he started to leave, Zac stopped him. "How are you getting home? Do you need a ride?"

"That's why I've got Easter here," Drake said, pointing to his pal, who in fact did bear a resemblance to one of the stone heads of Easter Island. Without a glance or word to anyone else, especially his stepmother, who had been sitting a few feet away the whole time, Drake left the house and Easter followed.

"What is it you're going to do, Zac?" Dane asked.

"I'm just doing him a favor," Zac replied. He avoided eye contact with any of us as he scurried away to his bedroom. "Don't worry about it."

In the lull, I noticed Mrs. Elliot was not present. I asked Ben where she was.

"She goes for a walk about this time every day," he said.

"Quig will be here soon," Dane snapped, venting her frustration and dislike of Drake upon me.

"Oh?" I replied.

"You're going to go to work with me, remember? I asked you last night."

"Yes, of course. I remember." I hadn't, but her impatient glance quickly reminded me.

DEATH TRIUMPHS

There were only two seats in the FCO van, occupied, of course, by Dane and Quigley, so I squatted behind the console between them. It gave me a clear view out the front. I balanced myself against a portable incinerator, which would be used later to destroy the hazmat suit I was sweating beneath at that moment, as well as all the needles, bandage tape, catheters, and other tools of the trade a civil attendant utilized. Prior to driving off, I had to remove all my clothes within a cramped dressing closet, just as Dane and Quigley had done, and put on the required scrub attire—under and outer layers, including shoes—that would be torched at the end of the appointment, when new attire would be donned. I chose to go without a mask. Dane gave me the "option" of wearing headgear—mask, respirator. It was regulation. But like with much of the FCO protocol, she took liberties.

"What we're doing is already hard enough on the families," she explained. "For us to be hooded and faceless only further impersonalizes it."

"We're not reapers," Quigley added.

"If incinerating our clothes and burning our skin off in a sterilization shower isn't enough to prohibit viral spread, then a mask or no mask won't make a shred of difference."

Behind me, the cargo area had a vague resemblance to an ambulance, neatly organized with medical supplies, yet comparatively sparse—taking a life didn't require as much inventory as saving one.

Although Samuel Elliot was the primary suspect in the release of the Omega, there remained skepticism and debate as to its origin. He was a minister, not a scientist. And was the disease strictly a manmade biological weapon, or was it an iatrogenic[†] form of something else? Or, in the case of one of the bolder proposals, perhaps it was both—that is, a *manufactured* mutation, a brilliantly designed, unstoppable weapon developed from HIV/AIDS, hepatitis, or a simple flu virus.

"Only man, or nature at its cruelest, could create such a thing," stated Dr. Philip Anderson—once the head of research at the University of California, San Francisco Medical Center—in an interview a week after the quarantine. "The virus has a triple threat in its makeup. It has shown itself to be airborne *and* blood-borne. Also, it can lie dormant in the body for months, as though waiting for just

---

[†] Illness borne of medical treatment, i.e., blackwater fever from treatment of malaria.

the right moment to take over. It's as though it thinks and behaves like a parasite, analyzing the most effective manner in which it can specifically adapt to the individual host. Even those who show to be immune at this time may not be in six months or six days. The virus is amazing in its ability to mutate, and frightening for the future of humankind. This could very well be our end."[†]

Thus, it earned the name Omega.

Its daunting attribute of lying dormant in a body for months before symptoms appeared had been a perverse blessing. Medications were developed that could retard growth of the disease in its early stages, giving patients a little more time while doctors desperately searched for a cure. Yet that only seemed to piss off the virus, as it would eventually mature with a vengeance to rapidly overwhelm the host beyond hope.

The early stages were marked by the innocuous signs of a cold or flu—fatigue, muscle aches, mild fever, and sore throat—before progressing to abdominal pain and tremors. Then, with the final stage, as nerve sensitivity was heightened and blood was coughed up, death soon followed. And a lot of death had followed.

The FCO, established as a cleanup squad comprised of "volunteers" known to be Omega-resistant, was able to do what other groups had failed to do—contain the spread of death. Of course, saying the others had failed wasn't exactly

---

[†] Dr. Anderson died from the virus two months after this interview.

fair; more accurately, they had died trying.

It began with medical professionals; then it was the Red Cross and a dozen other rescue organizations, all of them falling victim right along with those they attempted to help. Police and firefighters were next. When a state of emergency was declared and quarantine enacted, the National Guard arrived to quell the rioting. But soldier and rioter alike dropped like skin from a leper.

"People like to tell me how fortunate I am, being immune," Dane told me. "Yes, how lucky I've been to watch friends and strangers die all around me. How blessed I feel to read the daily death list and not see my name among the hundreds."

Along with being resistant, Dane was also "fortunate" enough to have been a veterinary technician. Experienced in the use of needles, the placement of IV catheters, and the administration of euthanasia, she was a prime candidate for the position of a civil attendant for the FCO.

"It's a strange thing to have on your résumé," she said, "being skilled in the efficient snuffing of little Fluffy's life."

I felt oddly fortunate myself, as I had the rare, unexpected occasion to accompany a team of civil attendants on the job. Dane drove the streets as though she owned them, steering us easily toward the Western Addition. It was a cool, overcast afternoon; like the day before, the avenues and sidewalks were thin with traffic and pedestrians. Quigley checked his GPS against the signal from the patient's bracelet.

"Are we getting close?" Dane asked him.

"Five more blocks—*mmrp*—on the left."

The primary duty of the civil attendant was to test for the virus. Like Nikki, most everyone living in the clean zone was biding their time for that final "negative" result so they could get out of the city. Or, like Mrs. Elliot, they could stay, assured that they were healthy, and ride out the storm until the quarantine was lifted. Their first call that day was for a subject whose bracelet had gone from green to orange, indicating a severe metabolic change.

A young, gaunt woman came into view ahead of us. She stood off the curb with one foot in the street and the other in the gutter, disturbing a trickling stream of water on its way to a drain. Her arms tightly wrapping her chest, the woman lifted her hanging head as Dane slowed and stopped the van. Quigley leaned over to his partner's open window.

"Mrs. Hernandez?" he asked her.

"That is my mother," she answered, her voice dull and weak.

"She's inside, then?"

"Yes, she's with my—" Grief strangled her words.

Quigley looked at the call order. "Daniel Hernandez? Is he your brother?"

The woman bit her lip, nodding. "He knew you would come. She didn't want to believe he was sick."

"What's your name?" Dane asked her.

"Angeline."

"Angeline, we're civil attendants with the Federal Coroner's Office. I'm Ms. Francisco, and this is Mr. Mason."

Per protocol, Dane and Quigley showed Angeline their credentials, and she carefully examined them. Dane also explained my presence there as an "authorized observer." If Ms. Hernandez had any objection to me watching, I would stay downstairs in the lobby, but the young woman nodded that she didn't mind.

She then allowed Dane to scan her (green) bracelet to certify her identity. Although we were in broad daylight and well within a clean zone, there were risks. Working for the FCO was a dangerous job (except for the position of an official bearer, whose duty it was to take away bodies— bearers are not protested or threatened with violence). Being on the street, attendants could be vulnerable to attacks, sometimes with fatal results. There were many people with strong opinions about the FCO's place in our society, and a few who took their opposition to vehement extremes. Verifying identification was one of the useful protocols.

Next, Dane gave a thorough visual search of the vicinity as Quigley gathered equipment. Once confident no one was lurking to ambush them, Dane said to the woman, "Mr. Mason is going to go into the building with you. Then he'll stay in the lobby, and you'll go upstairs and wait with your family."

"It's just me and my mother and my brother."

"Then you should be with them."

Quigley was out of the van at that point, a supply pack over his shoulder, leading Angeline toward the apartment building. He delicately explained the process and how nothing was certain until the test was performed.

Protocol said to park the van in an inconspicuous place, but Dane always left it double-parked on the street, as close to the entrance as possible. "Whoever made up *that* rule never had to get out of a situation," she explained. (A Dane Francisco fail-safe: know when it is important to flush protocol!)

She did one more check of the area, grabbed her own supply pack, then turned off the motor and got out of the van in a jog, with me only a step behind. Quigley was waiting for us, holding the lobby door open.

Our destination was on the second floor and down a narrow corridor. Onlookers lined either side of the hall, peering out from behind medical face masks. While the presence of civil attendants was sadly commonplace, our spectators watched intently. The *wisp-wisp-wisp* of our hazmat suits the only sound, the three of us walked past them. Then a voice came from behind.

"Reapers!"

Quigley took a sharp turn upon our audience. "What was that? I didn't catch that!"

It may have been his unnerving stature that kept everyone silent, or perhaps the comment had come from someone not really looking for a fight but merely letting go their frustration with the utter hopelessness. Either way, no one moved, and nothing more was said.

Satisfied, Quigley joined Dane, who was waiting at the Hernandez apartment. She lightly tapped on the door. It was the next one over that opened, however, giving Dane a start. A round old woman stepped out into the hall.

"He's a decent young man," she said, taking Dane's wrist with a gentle squeeze.

"Yes, ma'am," Dane said.

"We'll take good care of him," Quigley stated.

Angeline opened her own door then. She stood to one side, allowing Dane, Quigley, and me to enter. The air in the apartment was thick with the warmth of space heaters and dozens of ceremonial candles. An area of the living room was sectioned off by sheets—paisley patterned with a border of brightly colored flowers—that hung from a cord stretched wall to wall. More candlelight flickered behind the sheets. Angeline pulled one aside, and there lay her brother. Next to him sat their mother.

It was supposed to be a routine blood test for Daniel Hernandez, age nineteen. Even though his bracelet was orange, it was obvious that a test was pointless. His skin was deathly pallid, and when he parted his lips to take a painful, stuttering breath, his bleeding gums were exposed. He was clearly in the final stage of the disease. Dane knew Daniel had only a few hours to live, with or without her and Quigley.

She introduced the three of us to Mrs. Hernandez, whose lack of response was disregarded; whether the woman couldn't understand Dane's Spanish or simply chose not to acknowledge their presence didn't matter. Dane and Quigley proceeded to set up their equipment, quietly, reverently.

Daniel was in the final stage of the disease, which meant that every nerve ending in his body would be hypersensitive. The slightest touch would be excruciating for him. Dane applied a topical analgesic to the area she would draw blood from for the test. All she needed was a few drops and fifteen minutes; the drops would be added to a solution, and the color it changed to would determine either a positive or negative result. As those long fifteen minutes ticked by, Dane gently rubbed more of the numbing ointment onto Daniel's entire hand. A minute later, she told Mrs. Hernandez that it was okay to hold it.

As expected, the solution turned red, indicating Daniel Hernandez was positive for the Omega virus. The next step in the protocol was to remove the patient as soon as possible from the clean zone. Angeline and her mother had three options: move Daniel out of the area, where he would agonize until he died; take him to a hospital for "treatment," which would relieve some of his pain but prolong the inevitable end; or Dane and Quigley could induce his death right then and there, and release him from his suffering.

Mrs. Hernandez chose elective release.

Dane's least favorite part was next. Not the euthanasia

itself, but the *paperwork*—the cold legal jargon and clinical explanation of the process. Family members had to understand every detail before they could sign on the dotted line and set the procedure in motion. Once that was complete, Dane applied a liberal amount of ointment to Daniel's arm, to facilitate the smooth placement of an IV catheter. Quigley monitored vital signs while Dane administered the intravenous solution.

She worked with efficient dexterity as she readied her tape, catheter, and bag of solution, with its connecting IV line. Finding an acceptable vein was easy because of the patient's considerable weight loss. Dane slipped the catheter into Daniel's arm, taped it in place, and attached the line in one smooth, seamless motion.

Although the FCO had been designed to suppress an out-of-control situation through the efficient collection and disposal of infected, potentially contagious cadavers, Dane saw it differently: "If we can be so compassionate when Fluffy is no longer walking or controlling her bowels, then what about our brother, sister, son, or daughter?" Dane felt that what she was doing was about much more than containment.

"*¿Estás listo?*" Dane asked the two women as she prepared to activate the flow of solution.

"*Sí,*" answered Angeline.

Mrs. Hernandez could only give a deep, heavy nod.

Complete administration of the blue euthanasia

solution (a color chosen for its soothing qualities) would take twenty to thirty minutes—a carefully administered overdose of barbiturates. The gradual delivery of the diluted drug gave patients and family members one last chance to change their minds; the process could be stopped halfway through without fatal results.

For patients who were conscious and whose throat was not yet swollen from inflammation—making swallowing difficult, if not impossible—there was the option of taking a series of five capsules. The pills worked progressively, in a manner similar to the IV administration; once the fifth pill was taken, there was no going back. Even the induction of vomiting wouldn't help.

In her time with the FCO, Dane had only been asked to stop an IV drip once. It was a few minutes into the procedure when a woman decided she wanted her sister to die a "natural" death. The sister's husband, aware of how much discomfort his wife was experiencing, pushed for the euthanasia. So Dane and her partner at the time waited in neutral silence as the woman and her brother-in-law argued. While they quarreled, the sister died.

Most people understood that when a victim reached Stage 4, there was no hope for survival, only suffering. Dane would even check the daily research reports before every shift, just in case there was some breakthrough medication of which she could inform the public or even take with her on a call. (Imagine the elation of a family if an attendant were to arrive at their home with a lifesaver as opposed to the dismal expectation.)

"He's been in so much pain," said Angeline. Her brother was getting a grave, comatose hush about him. More than half the solution was gone.

"Don't worry," Quigley said, "he won't hurt anymore."

I had never seen someone die before. When my father passed on years ago, he was hundreds of miles away, and I hadn't seen him for some time prior. The news of his passing was like a belated farewell, and when I viewed him in the mortuary, I felt as though I were looking at a wax figure, an artificial representation of his body, face, and hands. I never had a sense it was my father; I already knew he was long gone. That made the ache of losing him manageable, even pragmatic.

I could only imagine the anguish Angeline and her mother must have been going through at that moment, witnessing a life so dear to them reach its end. To me, Daniel looked to be falling asleep, as peaceful as he would have been taking a Sunday-afternoon nap; it was only the knowledge that he would never wake up that caused my stomach to tighten.

But his mother and sister knew better. They knew they would never hear his voice or his laugh again; they were all too painfully aware that he wouldn't be there beside them to touch, to hold, to tease or bicker with, or to share a lifetime of experiences.

Dane watched closely as the last of the fluid flowed from the bag, through the venoset line, to Daniel's arm. She turned to Quigley as he verified the vitals once more. His nod told her that Daniel Hernandez was dead.

"He's gone," said Dane.

For many, that moment released all that had been swelling within—denial, anger, sorrow. Emotions ruptured forth, as they did with Mrs. Hernandez. She cried out, slid from the chair to her knees, and laid her head upon her son's chest.

For others, like Angeline, there was only relief. No more tears. No more words. Only silent thanks that her brother's agony was at an end.

Quigley solemnly collected their gear. Dane explained to Angeline that official bearers would be along within the hour to take away her brother's body. Also, she and her mother would have to be tested within the next twenty-four hours and possibly moved to an isolation zone. The young woman waited by the door, anxious for us to leave. The three of us walked past her. Dane could see Quigley was about to make some kind of consoling remark. She quickly took his arm and led him out.

We exited the building. Dane started the van's engine and unlocked the doors with her remote. Once in the van, she immediately shifted into drive and sped away. Dane never felt safe until she was moving.

"That whole building will have to be locked down and

every resident tested," she said with resignation. Then she asked Quigley, "Where to next?"

"The Hollow. Filbert and Scott," he answered.

Dane looked at me in her rearview mirror. "Well, what did you think of that?"

"I thought it was only an orange alert," I said.

"These things," she said, shaking her bracelet, "are only ninety-six percent accurate."

"So there's a four percent chance a green is really a red and vice versa?"

"Yep. Only a blood test is one hundred percent, even if there's a mutation." Then Dane turned to her partner. "How do you think it went?"

"I thought it went okay, huh?" Quigley commented.

"It could've gone better," Dane answered.

"How so?"

"That little scene in the hallway?"

"I just wanted—*mmrp*—to shut the punk up."

"We're lucky everyone in the building didn't snap us into the bay. There's always going to be some gump calling us out. If you challenge him, you might find he's got a bunch of friends behind him. There's nobody behind us, Quig. Nobody."

"We're not reapers," Quigley muttered defensively.

"Ignoring them would have done just as well. And you have to be careful how much you say to the family. Like when we were leaving. Saying nothing is always better than saying something stupid, or worse," Dane explained.

"Even words of comfort?"

"One person's comfort is another's annoyance. You never can tell. She just wanted us to leave. Sometimes it's best not to say anything."

Quigley began to say something in his defense, but Dane went right along.

"After doing my job one night to a woman in her sixties with her elderly parents in attendance, I tried to console them. The mother, especially, was uncontrollably upset. I think I said something like, 'She had sixty years of good life, which is more than a lot of people can say.' Well, the old man shredded me a good one." Dane continued, characterizing the voice of a crazed senior citizen. "'Good life? What the hell do you know about it? Her life was hell! Her husband abused her, her kids hated her, and she lost her job! And none of it for no good reason!' Blah, blah, blah! Hell, hell, hell!" she finished in her own voice. "He must've gone off for ten minutes. I couldn't pack up my equipment and get out of there fast enough."

Quigley responded with a feeble *mmrp*. Then he asked Dane to pull over so he could grab a coffee.

While we waited for him, I asked Dane, "Does that slight noise he makes spark your synaesthesia?"

She blushed, looked away with a sly grin, and I had the answer, which I already knew (because I had snooped through Ben's journals). Seeing her relax, I asked, "So, how do agents disconnect, like Quigley said last night?"

"I don't know. You'll have to ask Quig," she answered. "I can't do it. But maybe my saving grace is that I am not really a happy person to begin with. It's just how I'm wired. You might say I've already got one foot in the pool of misery we're festering in here. It's easy to deal with when you don't have any ideals to disillusion."

"You must have some opinion about what you do."

"Everybody dies. But not everybody has to suffer, I guess. It's best for everyone—victims, their families, and the uninfected population. Sometimes I wonder if we don't wait too long before we do our job. Maybe this thing would go away faster if we acted sooner."

Dane was wrong; she had ideals. And I believe she cared too much, like the soldier, Barthram, in Gohr's novel. Would it, too, be *her* downfall?

*　　*　　*

We went to eight more appointments that evening, two of which came to the same end as Daniel Hernandez. One of them, like Daniel, was younger than me. The other was a mother who, just a week before, had watched her husband and two children die without assistance; she went with only Dane, Quigley, and me beside her. It was an average day, according to Dane. She and Quigley then finished their shift at the Parnassus location of the University of California Medical Center, the hub of Omega virus research. They restocked supplies, emptied their incinerator, and performed personal sterilization procedures, of which I also had to participate. Cleanup protocol involved showering with an astringent, lathering antimicrobial chemical, followed by a nearly scalding rinse and then drying beneath infrared heat lamps.

The three of us took public transit home, Dane and I on one route, Quigley on another. It was dark out, but curfew was still over an hour away. The only passengers on the bus, Dane and I rode west on Lincoln Way, with Golden Gate Park to our right, toward Sunset Boulevard, which would take us home. I noticed an increased number of military patrols in the area, and Dane explained it was because of the park's allure to gangs, the homeless, and thrill seekers flirting with trouble.

"Thrill seekers?" I asked.

"There's a cult of idiots out there that plays a kind of truth-or-dare game where they challenge each other to cheat disaster. They say it makes them feel alive—you know, invincible, immortal." There was a tone of disgust in her voice that made me glad I wasn't one of them—or was I? "I think getting through the day here is enough of a challenge."

"Sounds a little personal," I mentioned.

She nodded. "I know a couple of those idiots."

The rest of our ride home was in silence. I wanted to learn more about the cult of idiots and the reapers, but I could tell she was shutting down; her day was done. Because the darkness outside prevented me from seeing anything but my own reflection in the window, I watched, instead, how Dane stared at the advertisements and graffiti above us. She didn't seem to be reading, but watching the colors that no one else could see.

At the house, everyone but Peter's mother was gathered to watch television. Mrs. Elliot offered Dane and me some spaghetti and meatballs that Zac had prepared; Dane was too tired to eat, but I helped myself to a couple servings. Then I slipped away to the bedroom so I could give Zac's recording an attentive listen. Moments later, before I could get started, Ben came into the room.

"How's it going?" he asked. "Have you come up with anything new?"

"No. Nothing," I told him. "I was just about to get back to it."

"I need a favor," Ben said as he closed the door quietly. "I'm going out with Zac after everyone's asleep. But—"

"You want me to lie to your mother?"

"Only if she asks, if she wakes up. Just keep this door closed and tell her I'm asleep."

"Where are you going?"

"Zac's got a favor to do for Drake. He's going to pick up Natyli from work at midnight. Drake's letting him use his car!"

"Who's Natyli?"

"Drake's girlfriend."

"That's so late. Where does she work?"

"The Fallout. It's a club."

I hesitated to agree to the scheme, wanting to stay uninvolved.

Then Ben said, "I'll let you read my journal. Maybe it will help you."

I paused, pretending to consider it. "All right...But be careful."

Ben stepped out of the room. I took my notebook in hand and pressed play on the tape recorder.

Through the buzz of static came that ghostly voice, faint at first, then clearer, and faint again. I played the tape as many as ten times, until I was able to make out a few more words than I had before. There were still gaps I couldn't discern, but in its entirety, the recording went as follows:

"...the written word—visceral, primal...to the earth, to each other...that we are, without...weekly sermon, it should be lived...then death triumphs...

"...church burn to the ground...construct by men within...building and the sacred texts...the smoldering embers, the smoke...I knew—that God was...then my belief became..."

By the tone of his voice, the speaker (Samuel Elliot?) seemed to be asking, even commanding, the listener to regain something lost. But what? Faith? A relationship with God? And there was that phrase again: "death triumphs." Was he saying grow spiritually and cheat death? In the second part, was he relating the experience of having watched his church burn down? But to what end? What happened to *his* belief? I couldn't put it together.

The dichotomy of opinions in the household didn't help, either. Mrs. Elliot felt her husband was innocent; Dane believed he could have done it. Zac thought his father was in South America, broadcasting sermons over the radio; Ben's conviction that his brother was wrong was undeniable.

The only commonality they shared was hope—the precarious hope that Samuel had no connection to the release of the Omega virus. They were like believers on the threshold of succumbing to the possibility of God's nonexistence, unable to take that last step and admit the intolerable truth for fear of being lost in a soulless world where death would surely triumph.

But what kind of man "mercifully" extinguished hundreds of thousands of lives? What in Heaven or Hell could have been his rationale? The answers had to be somewhere in his teachings. Zac's choppy recording wasn't nearly enough. My next best bet was the pile of notebooks that were Ben's journal. I had a lot of reading ahead of me, especially now that I had his permission.

GOD HATES COWARDS

"We're lucky the Omega originated where it did. Because of San Francisco's geological placement, it has been easier to lock down than, say, Los Angeles would have been."

While this quote from Congresswoman Anji Marhandi of California ruined her bid for re-election the following year, it expressed a sentiment that much of the country shared. (The general public only heard the first part of the statement—translated as, "We're lucky more than half of San Francisco was wiped out"—rather than its pragmatism as a whole.) However, those actually living in the Bay Area held a view more aligned with stand-up comic Vinny Rogers's perspective: "Bend over. It's time for an injection of *you're screwed!*"

In his journal, as he had in his blog, Ben outlined San Francisco's recent history. I found it helpful, as the sequence of events could often be muddy.

What started as a logistical nightmare turned into an exercise in controlled chaos.

For the most part, historically, times of disaster have brought about genuine altruism within and between communities. In the aftermath of San Francisco's 1906 earthquake, for example, people allowed strangers into their homes for shelter and food.

But such events also ignite fear and violence, wherein police and military act with a force that ripples through the population; the most minor incident (when fueled by the media) can easily overshadow the purest measure of humanitarianism. Thus is the case with this city's current history: the desperate cruelty of a few sending the goodwill of the rest into turmoil.

It actually began before the plague, a decade earlier, when extreme fundamentalist sects had fallen upon the Bay Area with a vehement mission: to bring deliverance to the decadence deemed so rampant there. As well as some "fringe" lifestyles in San Francisco, there was the full legalization of marijuana in California. Soon the recreational drug was being (illegally) laced with the hallucinogens POGO[†] (the joints called POGO sticks), or "u-phora," and thus the dawning of a new psychedelic era.

In response to the fundamentalists, a small secular faction attacked the "lies and judgments of self-righteous organizations" and protested the extent to which religious leaders had infiltrated and influenced the political machine. These nonreligious factions became known, informally, as

---

[†] A propofol glycol derivative.

Cross Hunters (Christianity being the primary target), but churches, temples, and mosques were vandalized and spiritual symbols were desecrated.

"My father isn't really surprised," Ben posted on his blog. "The Second Coming hasn't come. Islamic radicals want to kill everyone, and the Judaea army front, who also wants to kill everyone, arrogantly touts their 'chosen' status. It's no wonder religion is under attack. Or, as Dad put it, people have lost faith in Faith."

Tension between the two sides grew to a volatile pitch. The fundamentalists' escalating condemnation of abortion and the gay community led to the first of several riots: two free health clinics were bombed, and a gay wedding party was hit with balloons filled with rancid pig's blood. The police were forced to step in with tear gas and rubber bullets to disperse the clashing mobs.

Then the plague came.

Despite the fact that the Omega was introduced upon the public by a dozen or more aerosol bombs going off simultaneously, the fringe communities were singled out once again, as the pervasive disease was thought to be a mutation of the past AIDS virus. There were incidents of assault on homosexual couples, more than one beating ending in death.

It was soon found, however, that the Omega was a viral beast all its own, spreading through the city like wildfire. Thousands were infected before it was identified, and thousands more were dying before the quarantine was enacted. Panic soon spread faster than the disease; waves of conflict and dissent washed over the city streets. Martial law was passed.

Feeling vindicated, the narrow-minded fundamentalists proclaimed the Apocalypse was upon us. This only further incited Cross Hunters, enforcers of the secular radicals, who had simply had enough of righteous rhetoric. An attack on a group of demonstrators, zealots demanding repentance before it was too late, ignited yet another riot.

Greater fuel for the fire came when information regarding the Shepherds of Prophecy, a group of religious activists with whom Samuel Elliot was known to associate, became public. It was said that *they* had set off the aerosol bombs and then gone into hiding, their current location unknown. Another group, Mother One, was also implicated weeks later. Even military intervention couldn't restore order after that.

Ironically, the more resistance there was to containment and control by the government, the more the city became divided into contained, controllable sectors. A segment of the population considered as the greatest risk, calling themselves Fades, seized the North Beach/Wharf neighborhoods. Other groups followed their example: the Chinese community barricaded themselves into Chinatown, and a violent coalition of gangs grabbed an area south of Market Street, near the city's financial center. They had all, conveniently, quarantined themselves.

Some semblance of peace was maintained throughout the city, but vandalism and aggression directed at religion could not be fully subjugated. The police could not control the Cross Hunters. No denomination was immune; no spiritual leader was safe. It became a mirror image of the puritanical witch hunts of old—with the faithful now being targeted as the atrocity to be feared and hated. It was less an attack on God than it was the crucifixion of those who used Him as a platform for intolerance and hypocrisy.

The only choice to suppress the violence, according to authorities, was to ban all religious activity for an indefinite period of time. While a person couldn't be cited for "worshipping," they could be arrested and charged with disturbing the peace or intent to instigate a riot.

"It is a kind of *spiritual* quarantine," wrote Ben. "But you can't keep people from believing. Especially people as stubborn as my father."

As a result, ministries went underground. Any clandestine location would do. People gathered in the back rooms of warehouses, secluded corners of darkened playgrounds, or simply someone's kitchen with thick curtains covering the windows.

The most common places were quiet, banal locales that didn't draw attention.

To those looking for such a place, there could be any number of signs to indicate a safe haven. A candle in an upper-story window or a rose bush with all but a single bloom snipped off was typical. More obscure symbols included a dead fish on the lawn, a house with every light on inside (curtains or shades drawn), and a dog tied to a post or tree, yapping away like a sideshow barker or a prophet on a soapbox.

For a short time, Samuel Elliot held meetings in his living room, but soon saw the risk to his family. He then converted his truck from a mobile automotive repair shop to a portable chapel.

About his father's ministry, Ben wrote the following:

His church was a moving van. The bed was carpeted and oversize pillows were strewn about for people to sit, and he would sit with them rather than at a pulpit. My father's idea of a sermon was more of an informal discussion.

He made it well lit and there was plenty of ventilation (although the smell of grease and motor oil never did go away). The outside may have appeared a dingy U-Haul, but once inside, his congregation felt they could gather safely. He had also installed a pass-through to the front so that he could communicate with the driver—when he had one. He drove the truck himself and then parked to have his talk. Often, I would ride along and serve as lookout. One of the best places to park was on the Great Highway, overlooking Seal Rock; the long stretch of road made for a clear getaway, if needed.

He always began by welcoming everyone and thanking them for their courage. His gratitude was genuine. He knew the risk they were all taking by meeting in the back of that shabby truck. Whenever he mentioned the danger, it reminded me to check the surroundings, searching for anyone or anything suspicious.

My father would begin his sermons the same way, by saying, "I don't have the answers, just questions like you. Together, we can figure things out." One of his favorite questions for newcomers was, "If we didn't have places of worship like churches, temples, synagogues, and mosques or any sacred texts like the Bible and the Quran, how would we believe? Would there be anything to believe in?" Or sometimes he would simply ask, "Would God exist without religion?"

He rarely gave time for a response before continuing. "Of course, the atheist would say that since God is man-made, well, no religion, no God. No belief system, then nothing to believe. That person would have a valid point, too."

Once, a young woman answered with, "How sad." I don't think she intended to be heard, but my father never allowed anyone to be ignored.

"Yes, how very sad!" he answered her. "And isn't that exactly what we've come to? Isn't that why we are in the back of this truck? Our religion has been taken away, hasn't it?"

Here he would stop and wait for those attending to respond. This was difficult for him because he didn't have patience for passive believers. Thankfully, someone would usually respond with something like, "But we can still believe," or "No one can take our faith."

This was his cue to say, "I'll go even one better. No one can take our knowledge. I, for one, don't blindly trust or hope for His existence. I know there is God. Without a particle of doubt, I know. I don't need Scripture. Yes, some of it is very beautiful, and its lessons are inspiring. But are we really lost without it? I don't need ritual. I don't need someone to stand at a podium and preach to me. I've learned of God's work by observing the natural world, like any physicist or biologist. I know as I've always known because it's right there in front of me, in front of all of us."

Never in the dozens of times I've heard that lecture did I look at the faces of those listening and see anyone who "knew," as my father did. They did need the words and the lessons to affirm their convictions. They all had doubts.

My father would see the doubt, and he would go on with, "Philosophers have debated for centuries. They either passionately disprove His existence or they passionately defend their religious conviction. But defining God is impossible. The image of a perfect being is beyond human comprehension; any description of our Lord is flawed by base anthropomorphism and biases. At best, our realization of God is only what we deem to be divine qualities. And who among us has truly pure, unbiased vision?

"Religion is only a means by which a culture chooses to believe and organize itself according to that belief. It is not God. And God doesn't need us to believe. With or without our systems, it doesn't matter. God would still be."

Here someone invariably asked, "How would we know?"

And my father was ready with his answer, which was the point of his lesson and the whole of his ministry. "The same way that civilizations since the first civilization knew—by the presence of something divine in the world around them and, most important, within them. If you can't feel it, well, then you can't. But that doesn't mean it isn't there. It just means that you're missing out on something quite wonderful, a peace and power beyond words and intellect, and far above debate."

I remember one time someone came back with, "That sounds like the rationale of someone who's lost the debate." He was a teen with sunken features and an abnormally large forehead, not someone you'd easily forget.

"I don't waste my time with debates," my father replied to him. "It's like trying to explain a tree's existence to someone when it's standing right in front of them. If they can't see it, what's the point?"

The teen came back with, "What's the point of explaining something that doesn't exist?"

My father immediately removed the young man from

the truck and drove us away. Insolence was something else he had no patience for. He also took no chances that the teen wasn't a Cross Hunter setting a trap.

The looming threat of extremists wasn't the only danger to Samuel's ministry. His idea of believing in God without the guidance of an organized system ("a concept he took no credit for originating," Ben noted) made him unpopular with many of his peers, as well as attracting the attention of followers with unstable motives, followers like the Shepherds of Prophecy.

The founders were a small band of university professors—a contradictory cohesion of scientists and theologians—who claimed their individual belief systems had let them down. Each defied convention in his or her own way, and they merged with the desire to create a new way of looking at the world. But they had lacked direction—that is, until they found Samuel Elliot and his church-on-wheels.

But according to Ben, his father never intended nor wanted to be their leader. Besides sitting in on his sermons, a few of them started appearing at the Elliot home:

Dad chased them away. I overheard him tell Mom that they couldn't be trusted, but he didn't exactly say why. In one of his sermons to them, Dad talked about how we were all the past of things to come. And he asked, "What kind of future do you want to be responsible for?" But he didn't think they were listening to him. He said that the Sheep Herders, or whatever they call themselves, only listen to the voices in their heads.

I don't know. He may not have trusted them, but sometimes I think Dad liked the attention.

Together with his blog, Ben's journal was proving to be invaluable. The house was quiet—the television was off, so Peter's mother had obviously gone to bed—and I was alone with pieces to the puzzle I had been sent to find.

I took a break to get a glass of juice from the kitchen. It was later than I thought, as Mrs. Elliot was asleep in her chair and there was no light coming from the other rooms. I wondered a moment how Zac and Ben could've slipped out without their mother knowing, but then, as Nikki had said, she probably did know. If so, how could she have let them go? Did she think that they were their father's sons and there was no stopping them? Perhaps, but something told me that what they were doing that night had nothing to do with Samuel's ministry.

I returned to the bedroom and resumed flipping through Ben's private thoughts. I searched for the lengthy entry I had glimpsed earlier that day, before the interruption of Drake's visit. Mostly, the entries were minor:

It was as beautiful a day as I'd ever seen. The sun cast long shadows beneath the blue sky like a painting I saw the other day. I think it was an Edward Hopper. It was easy to convince the others to go see the seals with me.

— — —

I remember Morgan very well. He used to bully us. I

remember how glad Zac was when he moved away at the age of eleven, before he was big enough to do us serious harm. I can't believe how huge he is now. I was relieved to see him smile and shake Zac's hand. He looked happy to see us.

———

I saw my first Mutt. They deliberately disfigure themselves with burns or cuts. I've heard some will break bones and force them to heal in horrible ways. The girl I saw had burns all over her face. When I asked her what happened, she said she'd done it to herself. She looked like a pretty plastic doll that had melted in the sun. She got off the bus before I could ask her why she would mutilate herself like that. What was the point?

———

I'm happy when Dane's happy. She'd had a good day today. No one tested positive, so no one had to die.

I eventually found what I was looking for. It was an entry about a visit to the zoo he had taken with Zac and their father:

I loved the zoo when I was younger. My imagination always ran a little wild, past the bars and glass of the exhibits, and the animals seemed to have a lot to say to me. The last time we went, Dad told us we should go because who knew how much longer it would be around. I didn't know what he meant and didn't really think about it at the time.

It was the first weekend the zoo was open since that gang had raided and let a bunch of the animals loose. I think one of them was attacked by a tiger or a monkey or something. Anyway, it caused the facilities to be shut down for a while.

Of course, as soon as we got inside, Dad began to lecture.

"The success of these exhibits is measured by the amount of natural behavior demonstrated by the animal or animals within. They must be made to believe they are in their natural habitat, or at least they must be comfortable in their given environment so that they behave as though they were actually in the wild. Understand? Natural behavior means success; unnatural behavior is failure."

I wonder sometimes, what is the natural behavior of humans?

"Don't you think that a zoo is really nothing more than an exhibition in cruelty?" he asked us. "And wouldn't the wasted lives of these creatures be better off extinguished?"

There was a new wolf exhibit. We sat for a while and watched the forest carefully, but we didn't see any.

"They're in there. Like God, you don't need to see them to know it. But they are in there."

Dad had something to say about every exhibit. At the lion house, he said, "Never trust someone who thinks that domestic cats are smarter than dogs. Dogs have a willingness to learn from us. They have an innate ability to serve others for a greater good. And they do it with incessant enthusiasm. To me, that's the sign of a higher being, a higher intelligence. Lesser beings merely survive; they are selfish and aloof and disregard the needs of others. Like a house cat. There's more to living than just surviving. Any dumb animal can survive." Sometimes Dad joked about stuff like that, but this time I couldn't tell.

We passed the primate center, and I heard him mumble something about "monkey condos." Then we sat on a bench and looked at the flamingos.

Zac and I heard a radio from a food stand nearby. It was playing that song "3 Wishes" by Hobo Love. It's about a boy who's given the opportunity to have anything he wants and only chooses whatever will make the girl he loves happy. I heard the song again recently and wondered why I ever liked it. Anyway, hearing it prompted me to ask my father what he would wish for if he had three wishes.

By of the look on his face, I could tell he didn't hear the song and had probably never even heard of it. It must have seemed like a pretty random question to him. But he thought about it.

Zac said he would wish to get rid of all the hatred.

Then Dad said, "A decision like that can't be rash. A wish for world peace is a noble one. But it's a monkey's paw, isn't it? What would be the consequences of such an idea? Overpopulation? A depletion of land, food, and resources? And then what—a peaceful end to our existence?

One could argue that a complacent, safe life is worse than one of challenge, violence, and pain. You know how essential predators are in nature, right? They maintain balance, whether that predator is a wolf, a microbe, or a human. So what's the balance of such a wish?"

Zac gave me a reproachful look for getting our father started.

"My first wish," Father continued, "would be for something that would force the peoples of the world together in a spirit of peace and compassion. It would have to be something that would wake people up, a tragic experience, a horror shared by all. Some kind of destructive event. But a kind of event without judgment where the innocent and the guilty, and the wise and the clueless are all equal victims. So my first wish would be for something like an earthquake, or an alien invasion, or a plague, one that would take out half the planet's population before the first hope of a cure.

"Then, vulnerable and weakened by the pandemic, the survivors would find solace and strength in creating a new world order built on communal, worldwide peace, selflessness, and newfound reverence for the lives and needs of others. The good news for the damned is the bond of hope it creates. That would be my second wish."

He closed his eyes and looked upward, as though he were wishing for all that right then and there. Zac and I looked around nervously to see if it might come true.

Then I asked him, "What would be your third wish?"

"Oh, that's easy," he said with a smile. "To play guitar like Stevie Ray Vaughn." (I heard a song by that Vaughn guy the other day on the oldies music station and understood what my father meant.)

As the three of us sat quietly looking at the flamingos, a young boy came running down a pathway beside us and chased off a few seagulls that had gathered. Then he picked up a handful of rocks and proceeded to throw them, one at a time, at the flamingos. The boy's father strolled up and laughed at his son's antics. Dad stood and walked over to the father.

"Do you think it's a good idea to encourage such treatment of those beautiful creatures?" he said to the man.

"You mean those damn lawn ornaments?"

"You know, those birds are an endangered species."

"Get shredded, pal!" The man put up a stiff arm to keep my father from getting closer.

Dad stepped away calmly, shaking his head, and sat back on the bench with us. I don't know about Zac, but I was a little nervous. A few minutes later, the obnoxious father took his obnoxious son to a nearby restroom. Dad told me and Zac to wait. Then he went into the restroom, too.

A moment later, there was a noise, like a shout and the sound of someone falling down. When Dad returned, he ushered us toward the main exit. I heard a child crying and the hollow echo of a moan coming from the restroom. I couldn't help but run back there before Dad could stop me. I peered inside the open door to the facilities. I couldn't see much, but I heard the sobbing. "Daddy? Daddy?" The father's only response was a muted groan. I could see his legs, limp upon the floor, sticking out from one of the stalls.

Dad took me by the shoulders and pushed me in the direction of the exit once again. "You will find in your life, Ben, that most people aspire to nothing more than human waste."

I told Dane later about Dad's three wishes. She responded with, "What a load of crap!" It was strange to see her so angry with him. Sometimes I think she loves him more than we do, like a protective daughter.

She went on. "There shouldn't be a caveat to having peace in the world. There's been more than enough suffering to validate it. Remember how he once said that 'God hates cowards'—you know, that we should face challenges. Well, I challenge the world to live peacefully. Try it! That's all I would wish for. That people find the strength to live in peace. Hell, someone would have to wish for it because it won't happen otherwise."

I kind of regret telling her about our zoo trip.

*   *   *

As I sat there in the silence of the earliest minutes of a new day, sorting through all I had heard on Zac's recording and read in Ben's journal, that same queasy trepidation I'd felt upon my arrival the day before returned. It wasn't Samuel

Elliot's beliefs, his ministry and practices, which were comforting in their clarity. It was his three wishes. (Two wishes, actually. I mean, who wouldn't want to play guitar like Stevie Ray Vaughn?) And it wasn't for the obvious reason that I felt so uneasy. What caused my heart to sink deep into my knotted gut was the fact that what Samuel Elliot wished for actually made sense. Mrs. Elliot was right when she'd said, "He made you believe because he believed." I was sick to my stomach because I believed him, and I agreed with him. Yes, Dane was right, too: humankind *had* fought and hated and suffered for too long. But we'd lost a reason to live. We needed a clean slate, a new beginning, even if that meant putting most of us out of our misery.

I grabbed my Moleskine and began to write down a flood of questions. Were the references to past and future in Samuel's teachings and the philosophy of the zoo residents a coincidence? Or was there a more direct connection? Were those living in the zoo once followers of Samuel Elliot? Could they be more than mere homeless people looking for shelter? Were they a cohesive group of faithful looking for refuge? Once the chaos subsided, would they emerge to carry on their new order?

I stepped from Ben and Zac's room with the disorientation of waking from a deep sleep. I needed to talk to Ben, but he wasn't home. Then I remembered—he had snuck out and gone someplace with Zac, to a club called The Fallout.

THE FALLOUT

Living normal, day-to-day lives. Establishing a foundation of routine. Going to the openings of new businesses and the reopenings of old ones. Distracting yourself with a good book or bad television. Letting go of inhibitions by marching in a parade. There was any number of ways people coped. And I would soon learn of one more method—playing "games."

Dane had spoken of a cult of thrill seekers that "plays a kind of truth-or-dare game," because, as she explained, "it makes them feel alive." For example, a game might be challenging someone to venture into an infectious neighborhood for a period of time—better yet, after curfew. As a participant, you could be dared to infiltrate the Halloween Procession and then get back out. Or you might be taunted enough to sneak into the zoo community and spend the night among its residents. To the "gamers," living in fear wasn't living, so they tempted each other's fate, putting one another in life-threatening situations, often without the foreknowledge of it happening. To Dane, they were cowards. "Why else would they have to prove they're *not*, again and again?" she would state.

No matter the opinion held about them—cowardly manipulators or adrenaline freaks—there were a significant number of participants throughout the city, from every walk of society. They were teens and twentysomethings, rarely older, with the common bond of needing to know there was more to life than merely waiting around to die. They were organized, and a few were even entrepreneurial in their own way. One such endeavor manifested itself into the form of a nightclub known as The Fallout.

It wasn't so much a nightclub, but a predesignated location to get together and party. The locale was never the same—an abandoned storefront, a warehouse, a residence, any place that had been stranded in the aftermath of the city's recent chaos—and the party would last as long as it would take for the police to arrive, sometimes an hour, sometimes a couple of days. Of course, it was always set within a restricted zone after curfew. Otherwise, where would be the danger?

One of the organizers of The Fallout was Natyli Daemon. An opportunistic young woman who had sworn to never work "the daily grind," Natyli had all the tools for ignoble success, from a pleasant façade to an unscrupulous core, uncompromising devotion to self-reliance. And what she lacked in "pretty" she more than made up for in sexual appeal. The girlfriend of Drake Phillips, Peter Miller's stepbrother, their relationship was by no means quaint; it was a partnership founded on mutual fear and loathing.

On the night Drake asked Zac to pick up Natyli from work (using Drake's car), The Fallout was staged in a small grade school south of Market Street, a few blocks from the deserted Yerba Buena Gardens and Muscone Convention Center. The school was made up of two two-story, building-block-like units, painted red and blue. An open walkway connected them; entrance into each classroom was done from the outside. A concrete playground lay between the buildings, and all was enclosed by an eight-foot iron fence.

Activities would begin shortly after curfew, after the police and military had done their initial patrols. Natyli would manage the party's start, but leave as soon as possible; she couldn't afford to be caught there, if or when the activities were discovered by authorities. As Drake had told Zac, she was going to leave at midnight that night, so Zac and Ben slipped out of the house while their mother slept soundly in her chair and I sat in their room reading through Ben's journal.

Drake's Specter was more car than Zac had ever driven, a powerful machine with precision and responsiveness that required a deft touch, which Zac did not possess. At his hands, the car lurched around corners, accelerated in jolts, and jerked to stops.

"You know where you're going, right, Zac?" Ben asked.

"It's programmed into the GPS," Zac explained as his

thin fingers strangled the steering wheel, "by a route that lets us slip through the barricade without notice."

"Drake thought of everything, huh?"

The key to getting to The Fallout was to drive fast and not to stop—to avoid law enforcement, of course, but also to escape the gangs. Having a party in their part of town was as much of a game to them as anyone taking the risk to attend. Armed guards[†] were posted around the chosen location. Once you arrived to the club, no problem; it was a safe zone, like in a game of hide-and-seek or tag. Outside the club, though, you were a free target, for no other reason than the fact that you were there.

Across the street from the school was a playing field that had become The Fallout's parking lot. Like the school, it was equally fenced in and guarded. Zac pulled up, finally able to wield Drake's car like a seasoned driver, and was directed to an available space by a muscle-bound attendant with formidable steel-blue weaponry strapped to his side. Zac and Ben were checked for identification and weapons, and then given a parking receipt, which they would have to redeem before being allowed back into the enclosed area to retrieve their car.

"No tick-ee, no car-ee," the attendant smirked.

Except for guards, no one was outside the classrooms— it would draw too much attention to what was going on

---

[†] *Illegally* armed guards, since there was a federal ban on civilian-owned guns as part of previous riot control.

there. (Although, it seemed the playground full of parked cars would have done just that.) Each classroom had something different happening within; there was something for everyone. There were game rooms. There were music rooms where you could perform, dance, or listen. There were rooms where you could fight in "refereed" contests. Of course, in every room, alcohol and marijuana were in abundance. In the cafeteria, you could eat and watch movies.

The most popular space was the VR room, where limitless computer-enhanced adventures awaited. A player could go to any time or place in the universe or visit realms beyond reality and imagination. For a significant fee, any of the programs could be downloaded with a sex mode.

Drake hadn't told Zac exactly how to find Natyli, so he and Ben randomly chose rooms to enter, look around, and leave. After several rooms, they were approached by a long, lean guard with a pockmarked face and big hands.

"You need to pick a room and stay there," he told them.

"We're looking for Natyli Daemon," Zac said.

"VR. That way" was the reply, with one of the large hands directing them.

The room was sectioned into office-like cubicles, each with its own VR chair and system. A few of the cubicles in the back of the room were completely enclosed for privacy. Every cubicle was occupied, and there was at least a dozen more people squeezed into a waiting area.

Natyli approached Zac and Ben, and every one watched

her. She was not a petite woman, but her curves were in all the right places; her swaying walk, eloquent and confident, her dark eyes, and her glistening black hair all commanded attention. "You're early," she said to the brothers.

"I-I wanted to be early," stammered Zac, "just in case." According to Ben, Zac was always awkward in the presence of strong women.

Natyli looked the two of them up and down, and said, "Well, it's going to be a bit. I'll be here a little later than planned. There's plenty around to keep you entertained. Meet me out front in a couple of hours." She began to slink away, but stopped and turned back to them. "Unless either of you want to spend a little time with me here. No extra charge." She gestured to the private rooms with a deep laugh.

Flustered, the two quickly blurted that they were hungry and left the room to find the cafeteria. In their search, they hoped they wouldn't run into the tall, big-handed guard again and have to explain why they were out in search of yet another room.

The cafeteria was packed, and the air was thick with the smell of ethnic cuisine and warm bodies. The farthest wall was an immense Holo-Vision screen showing a loud action movie that no one was really watching. True to the room's functional design, food was laid out as a buffet. Zac and Ben grabbed trays, silverware, and plates and shuffled along with the slow-moving line to the smorgasbord of choices. To better show the movie, the lights were low. "Which was a blessing," Ben later explained. "I don't think I would've wanted to eat if I could have seen the food too well."

Their next challenge was to find a place to sit. After minutes of roaming the narrow aisles between tables, Zac decided they would simply squeeze into a pair of spots that offered just enough space for their trays. With the distractions of energy and activity around them, no one else at the table seemed to notice or care.

Although it was the Halloween season, Zac and Ben were not surrounded by eccentric people playing dress-up—it was all real. There was nothing costume about the makeup, as thick and glittering as it was; the studs on a lot of the jackets were not tin or plastic but steel, with edges as sharp as knives. For every person who was there to have fun, there was one looking for excitement, looking for a fight. To them, violence was the fun. Like the goon Zac made eye contact with at a nearby table. Zac smiled a greeting at him and went back to his meal.

"What are you smiling at?" the goon shouted through the crowd and over the blare of the movie.

With an evasive shrug, Zac replied, "Just being friendly!"

The goon then shouted to someone at another table. "The fag with AIDS wants to be my friend!" (Simpletons referred to Fades—that portion of the city's population considered the greatest risk—as "fags with AIDS," though there was no evidence that the Omega had any connection to the once widespread HIV virus.)

Zac's new friend and two others approached. All three had their hair greased back into a long point that extended halfway down their back. They wore tattered green leather trench coats and matching boots. The shortest and most muscular of them—his upper arms and shoulders about to tear through his leather sleeves—pushed through the slow-moving crowd like a beast from the jungle. He went through a series of fierce and threatening poses in front of Zac, who could only stare, dumbfounded.

"Man, he won't even throw a punch," one of them remarked to the others.

Ben looked around for a security guard, an escape route, or something he might use as a weapon besides the dull eating utensil in his hand. Zac turned back to his meal in hopes the three of them would get bored and go away.

But that's exactly what they wanted him to do. They moved closer and positioned themselves around him. Then the muscular one grabbed Zac and pulled him from his seat. It was there that Zac's wiry build proved its use as he slipped from the goon's hold and escaped the rest of them by twisting his way into and through the crowd. Ben did his best to follow. But just as he had done with me at the zoo, Zac cut his own path, only regarding himself, not once looking back for Ben.

Their hulking pursuers lumbered behind, quickly losing sight of the two brothers, who in fact had circled around and came back from the rear. Zac and Ben followed the leather-clad trio from a safe distance, keeping them in view. Suddenly, a fourth goon, bigger than any of the others, came up behind *them*. He grabbed the two with a viselike grip and let out incoherent but very excited cries. The others turned and tore back through the crowd.

As soon as they were close enough, Zac let lose a kick to the nearest one's knee, and Ben turned his teeth upon the hand that held him, drawing blood from the fleshy part between the thumb and forefinger. Both goons screamed like children, and Zac and Ben made a move to escape once again.

They only got as far as a pair of onlooking security guards. What the guards had witnessed were a couple of rowdy punks running crazy through the crowd who, when subdued by a pair of concerned patrons, proceeded to kick and bite. With an event as volatile as The Fallout, control had to be maintained, and there were examples to be made. Zac and Ben fit the bill and were swiftly escorted from the premises—not just from the cafeteria or the building, but the entire school grounds. They were taken outside the security fence and into the street; their attempts to explain or apologize ignored.

The street was a narrow lane between the school and the playing field turned parking lot. For the moment, it was quiet and empty—beyond the goings-on within the school. The brothers knew, however, it wouldn't be long before they would have unwanted company, and outside the perimeter of the school or the parking area, the security guards would be of no help. Those were the rules.

"The car," Ben said. "We can wait in the car."

They hurried to the parking lot's gate, Zac digging frantically through his pockets for the receipt. He gave it to the attendant, who was different from the one who had admitted them, but equally intimidating.

"This is a good idea," Zac said while they waited for the attendant to return. "We'll just stay in the car until it's time to go."

The attendant returned with a bemused and not amused look on his face. "Nice try, friend," he said, the parking receipt crumpled within his enormous fist.

"What are you talking about? Give us our car," Zac replied, his pitch intensifying to a whine. "We need our car."

"There's no car in this stall. Now, move on."

Neither brother could speak or breathe. They ran around the outside of the parking area in a frenzy, looking through the fence for Drake's Specter.

"It should be right there!" Zac cried, pointing to an empty space near the middle of the lot. "That's where we parked, that space right there!"

Again, Ben kept his head. He searched the streets, the alleys, and the shadows for an answer or a way out. Zac, on the other hand, was climbing halfway up the towering fence, determined to go up and over.

"Get down from there!" shouted the attendant as he approached from safe inside the lot. "Even if you make it, I'm just going to throw you out of here!"

"What did you do with our car?" Zac cried from above. His fingers were losing their grip, and his feet struggled to maintain support of his trembling frame. He shook the fencing with the last of his strength. "Where's our car?"

Zac lost his foothold. His hands were unable to hold his weight on their own, and he dropped like a sack of wet laundry—a sack of wet laundry with flailing arms and legs, that is. He landed with a lifeless thud, and for a moment, Ben thought his brother was unconscious or dead, until he heard him moaning and cursing into the hard ground. Ben also heard the attendant laughing as he walked away.

"Come on, we have to find someplace where we can wait for Natyli," Ben said to Zac, "someplace where we're not so visible."

Zac continued to lie still, right where he had landed.

Ben leaned over him and placed a hand upon his shoulder. "Zac?"

"Yes, yes," Zac replied as he rolled onto his back, "I'm alive."

It took him a number of steps to work out the aches from his fall, but soon Zac was moving right along with Ben's quick pace in search of a shadowed hideaway. They made their way to a dimly lit area near the parking lot. If anything, they could hide within the darkness. They got closer and saw it was a neighborhood playground; the blackened outlines of a swing set and a jungle gym became visible.

The brothers hunkered between a tree and a garbage can, with a partial view to the spot where Natyli would meet them. Sounds of The Fallout seeped through the night to their chilled ears, and both of them were painfully aware of being watched.

"How much longer, I wonder?" Zac whispered.

"At least another hour, I think," answered Ben.

"No. An hour?"

"At least."

"We can't stay out here for an hour."

"Come up with something better, and we'll do it," Ben responded impatiently.

The two of them caught their breath at the sound of a voice from behind. "You can hide in here, if you want," it said. It was a woman's voice, empty and estranged.

Neither Zac nor Ben moved, thinking they had somehow imagined it. Still, they readied themselves to run.

"I trust you," the woman said.

But did the brothers trust *her*, whoever she was? They turned to see the dome-shaped jungle gym was covered in cardboard and blankets, an urban igloo of cloth, paper, and steel. Through the darkness, they could only guess the voice had come from there. Then the woman leaned her head out of an opening that served as the abode's entrance.

"Come on, come on," she said, "before someone sees

you."

Ben admitted to us later, "I don't think I ever felt more vulnerable than when Zac and I crossed the short distance between our garbage can's shadow and that woman's sad dwelling. It was only about twenty feet, but the exposure we felt was petrifying."

As they entered the "igloo," the woman briefly shined a light, only long enough to show them that she was alone and they would be safe. It was also enough time to glimpse the hard, angular shape of her face and the grisly scar running from above her left eye, through her cheek, to her chin. It wasn't self-inflicted, like a Mutt, Ben thought to himself; someone had done that to her.

"I've been watching you," she said. "I thought you could use some help."

"Thanks," Ben replied. "We appreciate it."

"You can stay here until my children get back."

"You and your children live here?"

"For tonight."

Zac and Ben stayed near the opening and watched. They had a clear view of the parking area, the attendant wandering within the fence, and part of the school. They could see security pacing the grounds and, occasionally, patrons moving from one classroom to another. No sign of Natyli coming out to meet them, though.

"What's going on in there?" the woman asked.

"It's a...party," Zac said.

"What the hell do they have to party about?"

"I don't know. Being alive, I guess."

The woman's laugh was hollow and void of humor. "I'm alive. You don't see me celebrating. If it weren't for my kids..." Her voice trailed off, wisped away by a cold wind that rattled the cardboard and fluttered the blankets of the shelter.

"You said you were watching us," Ben said to her. "Did you see who drove away in our car?"

"I've watched a few come and go in the past half hour, but I don't know your car," she answered.

"Who took our car?" Zac mumbled to himself.

Ben had a strong suspicion of who had done it, and he couldn't figure out why his brother didn't share the same feeling. He had no intention of telling him, though; he wanted Zac to come to the logical conclusion all on his own. Ben turned back to the woman and asked, "How many children do you have?"

"Four," she answered. Ben could barely make her out; she was just a voice in the night. "They're out looking for something to eat."

"Safer to go out at night, is it?"

"What?" was the confused reply.

Ben gathered that it was never safe to be out around there.

Always the minister's son, he was genuinely interested and concerned for the sad woman and her children. And she seemed to welcome his questions about her life and circumstances. It became apparent to him that the woman in the igloo was in need of someone to talk to.

"My husband lost his job. Then he got sick," she told Ben. "I'm immune—the children, too. But it doesn't matter. We were forgotten about when they began to move people around. Now we're stuck here, living like animals. We scrape whatever food or clothing we can from the streets. My children can't even go to school. Every day, I go to the wall and ask them to let us through, but we're sent away. I don't have money to pay a 'spook.†'"

It was then that Ben noticed her green bracelet.

"You should be living in the zoo," Zac stated flatly.

"What?" the woman said. She didn't understand the reference; she probably knew nothing of the zoo community, Ben thought. Then she continued. "We should be living in another state, far away from here. No one healthy should be living anywhere near here. This whole city needs to be condemned until the sick are all gone. And then burn it to the ground."

Her lament was interrupted by the distant sound of sirens and the glow of flashing red-and-blue lights, rapidly getting closer. People began to flood out of the classrooms in a mad escape. They rushed down the steps, across the concrete playground, and through the gate to the street.

---

† Someone who sneaks others from an infected zone to a clean zone for a substantial fee.

Most took off running, while a few fought to get their cars out of the parking area. The attendant was gone as fast as anyone, leaving the gate open to a lot filled with automobiles. One driver didn't bother with the proper exit but instead tore through a weak section of fence, which brought one entire side of the steel-mesh structure down upon a row of cars.

"That's 'dise," Zac muttered in amusement. Hidden within their shelter, he and Ben were invisible to the pandemonium. The shouts and cries of panicked partiers were overwhelmed by the sirens. The neighborhood was awash in a strobe of red and blue. There was also laughter and shrieks of excitement, as though it were all part of the game, the only rule being to stay alive and not get caught.

"That has to be the shortest Fallout yet," Zac commented.

"I think I see Natyli," said Ben.

It was easy to spot her amid the disorder—she was the only one not running hysterically, a leather bag casually hanging from her shoulder. She walked in the direction of Zac and Ben with the seductive composure of a runway model or a star in command of the red carpet, while the event she had put together spiraled out of control around her. Zac called out to her. His sudden appearance from the jungle gym had no effect on her poise.

"What the hell are you doing?" she responded.

"We're in here," he told her. He made a motion for her

to follow him inside, but Natyli was not one to crawl into holes.

"Get the car. Let's get out of here," she demanded.

"It's gone."

"What's gone?"

"Drake's car. Someone took it."

Natyli looked down at Zac. Then at Ben. Then at the parking lot and its partially collapsed fence, the school, and the approaching trucks with their sirens and lights. Then back at Zac.

("She looked at him," Ben later explained, "with such a glare of contempt like I've never seen from anyone. It was chilling. All I could think was that 'I'm glad she isn't looking at me.' And I felt bad for my brother because he hadn't figured it out.")

"What's the matter with you?" Natyli said. Her voice was taut in its vehement restraint. "Are you cranked? Retarded? Or just fucking stupid?"

All were questions for which she didn't expect answers. Still, Zac tried to respond. He stammered and looked away as though the right words were etched into the sidewalk or written upon the cardboard wall of the shelter

"Drake took the car!" she shouted. "He set us up! Look!" She pointed to the emergency vehicles, which were now in clear sight and moving past the school. They weren't police or military, but a pair of common pickup trucks fitted with sirens and flashing lights and driven, most likely, by some of

Drake's friends. They laughed and hollered as they crept along, shining spotlights over the area in search of victims to scare and chase. The moment their beams fell upon Natyli, she pulled a gun from her bag and began to shoot at them. She hit one of the lights, putting it out with a burst and a flash, and continued to fire at both vehicles as they sped away.

The trucks were moving out of view, their sirens echoing along the empty streets. They were an appropriate soundtrack to Natyli's rant: she cursed Drake, ripped into Zac, reprimanded her inept security staff, sent a few expletives Ben's way, and even panned the pitiful jungle gym shelter! (Ben remembered the woman with them. He looked, but she was no longer there.)

"Are you getting it now?" Natyli said to Zac. "He stuck us here without a way home!"

"We could start walking," Ben boldly suggested. "It's less than five blocks to the wall."

"You're as stupid as your brother. We'd be lucky to make it two."

"You do have a gun, don't you?" Ben said.

Natyli looked at the weapon in her hand as though having forgotten it was there. "Well...yes." Then with a tone almost resembling embarrassment, she added, "I fired off all my rounds at those fuckers."

"Then maybe the sight of it will be enough. I say we start walking."

"No, wait," interjected Zac. Ben didn't like the look of his brother, a shroud of desperation settling upon him. "We can take one of those cars over there."

"Since when can you jack a car?" Ben asked. Zac didn't respond, but Ben already knew the answer: never.

Zac looked into the first vehicle he came to (a sleek Italian model), grabbed a fair-size rock, and smashed the driver's window. The alarm that went off was louder than any of the sirens that had just faded into the distance. Its shriek forced Zac to cover his ears and sprint back to the playground.

"That's great!" Natyli shouted over the alarm. "Now the police *will* be here! We need to get the hell away!"

"Zac, give me your phone!" said Ben as he moved farther back into the shelter. "I'm going to call Dane!"

*   *   *

As I stepped from Ben and Zac's room in my disoriented state, Dane was in the hallway, about to knock on my door. "You're awake," she said. "I just got called in, an appointment that can't wait. I thought you might want to come along."

I gathered my thoughts and glanced at my watch. "I don't know that I can do that," I said.

"Don't worry. We're exempt from the curfew. If you're with us, you'll be okay." She could see that I wasn't all there. "Quig is picking us up, so you have a few minutes to get yourself together."

"Yes. Of course I'll go."

By the time Quigley showed up in the van, I was in a fidgety state. I knew we would stay within the clean zone, but the idea of being out after curfew was still exciting and a little frightening. This time Quigley drove. Another late cloudburst made for a dank night, and the tires of the van hissed along the drenched, empty streets. I commented on the eerie absence of police and military patrols.

"They can't be everywhere," Dane replied. "They concentrate on trouble areas, like south of Market. It also gives the rest of us a sense of normalcy."

"Don't want to upset the natives," Quigley added.

I caught a glimpse of three darkened figures ducking into the shadow of a building as we rolled past. The bright light of their bracelets pierced the night; any attempt made to cover them with the cuff of a sleeve was pointless. "What happens if they find you out after curfew?" I asked.

"Nothing usually," Dane said. "You get scolded and escorted home."

"It depends on who you are and—*mmrp*—what they think you're doing."

The stat call they were responding to was from a young girl's parents who could no longer watch their daughter suffer. Quigley pulled up to a house that had been taped off from the other houses in the neighborhood. That didn't prevent a crowd from gathering at the front door and down the walkway to the street, however. The complete disregard to the quarantined home and the risk to the health and wellness of everyone gathered there was at once disconcerting and touching. The girl of concern was loved, selflessly, by many people.

"This is going to be hell to isolate," commented Dane.

She went through the protocol with the girl's father. He had trouble focusing and answering her questions. Dane apologized for the formalities, and as soon as he signed the last document, she encouraged him to wait inside with his daughter. Before exiting the van, Dane looked again at the call order, which noted that the family had previously refused euthanasia when the girl "went red" three weeks prior.

"This whole block should have been contained," Dane said.

We made our way through the entourage of mourners, who parted to allow us into the humble home. There was an air of courtesy in their whispers, and many of them thanked us for being there. I could tell it left Dane a little uncomfortable (she admitted later that their kindness made her feel vulnerable and, somehow, not in control), but Quigley seemed to be enjoying the positive attention.

Inside, it was bright and clean; it felt like a hospital, or after a closer look, like a chapel. Plaster base-relief cherubs adorned one wall, and a painting of the Madonna and images of Christ—the Sermon on the Mount, the crucifixion, the resurrection—covered the others. It was not a household that shielded its faith. Rather, their belief was a shield that strengthened and protected. They wore it proudly, like armor, and dared anyone to try and take it away.

The girl, Bethany, lay in a bed in the living room. This allowed for as many people as possible to gather around her. Above the bed hung a framed cross-stitch of Ephesians 5:14: "Awake thou that sleepest, and arise from the dead, and Christ shall give thee light." I wrote the passage in my notebook next to Samuel Elliot's "Hope is the fallout of despair."

Again, the mourners parted so that Dane and Quigley could approach and do their work. The girl had a dull, colorless complexion, and there was an unsettling odor in the room, attributed to something other than a lot of people crowded together. Dane placed a hand to the girl's face—she was as cold as stone. The poor well-loved girl had been dead for hours, and no one seemed to know it.

Dane did not let on to the truth, not even to Quigley, whose attention was on setting up for the procedure. She continued with experienced fluidity, and the crowd moved closer as she worked. There was crying, and from someone in the back came the gentle murmur of a prayer. Dane paused, as though drawn to its soothing tone, and then performed an abbreviated procedure, cutting it short before anyone could see that the solution wasn't exactly flowing into a vein, but collecting just beneath the skin.

"She's gone," Dane stated quietly as she wrapped a

gauze bandage around the discolored area of Bethany's arm.

Quigley realized what had happened and followed Dane's lead to pack up and leave. The group made space for the three of us to leave; we were allowed to easily slip past the crowd.

When we reached the van, Dane said, "Can you believe all these people? I'd be lucky to have one person at my funeral."

"Don't say that," Quigley replied. "You know I'd be there—*mmrp*—and I'd bring my dog, Simon."

I had never seen Dane give a broader smile than she did at that moment. Whether it was Quigley's energetic good looks, his humor, or the way his verbal tic made her see colors, it was clear her affection for him was growing. I couldn't help but feel I was intruding.

A breeze stirred between the three of us, bringing with it a woman's timid voice. "Excuse me. Excuse me?"

"Yes?" Quigley said, turning to her.

"Can you help me?" Her appearance was as indistinct as her speech, invisible, unmemorable. She had the figure and features of a thirty-year-old, with the sunken eyes of an eighty-year-old.

"What can we help you with?" Quigley asked.

"My mother is sick."

"How long has she been sick?"

"Her band turned orange this morning."

With his best bedside manner, Quigley said, "Orange is

only an alert. She needs a blood test to verify her condition." He checked his handheld. "We haven't received any other signals for this area."

The woman was clearly frustrated and confused. Dane piped up. "It's okay. We can do it. Sometimes a bracelet can be wrong." She put a gentle hand to Quigley's arm, then moved in closer to the woman. "Where is your mother?"

The woman glanced at the crowd of mourners behind us. For a moment, she looked as though she were about to change her mind, but she turned and led us to a bungalow a few houses up the street.

While the previous scene was sad, it was still warmed by love and devotion for the young girl. However, the dark, cold home of the woman and her mother was sad and nothing more. In a recliner in the front room sat the mother. She was in her sixties, with flowing silver hair. She appeared weak, and her breathing was labored. As her daughter had said, her bracelet was orange.

"This is your mother?" Dane clarified with the daughter, who nodded, looked away, and moved off into a corner. "What's her name?"

"Diana."

I hovered just inside the front door, hesitant to fully enter the uninviting home. Dane and Quigley approached the woman.

Dane knelt beside the recliner and placed a hand upon her shoulder. "Diana? I'm Ms. Francisco with the Federal

Coroner's Office. Can you hear me?"

The woman nodded and forced a dull groan, all the while keeping her eyes closed.

"How are you feeling right now?"

"Tired. I'm so tired," Diana answered.

"You're in pain?"

Diana could only muster the strength for another moan.

"Where's the pain? Where does it hurt?"

Again, she didn't speak, but pointed to her chest and clutched at her blouse.

Dane asked Quigley for a test kit. The daughter remained across the room as Dane informed Diana that she was going to take some blood. During the time while the test processed, Dane examined her. When the test and examination were complete, she went to the daughter.

"Your mother has tested negative for the virus," she told her. "Except for apparent fatigue, she seems to be healthy."

"I know," the daughter stated with a guarded tone. "She isn't sick in that way."

"I don't understand. What's wrong with her? How is she sick?"

The woman paused to choose her words, then simply said, "She doesn't want to live."

It was hard to read Dane's face. Past the confused, furrowed brow, something was brewing. "I'm sorry? So...she's depressed? And she doesn't want to live?"

"Yes, she was diagnosed. And then this morning her

wristband changed color."

"She's clinically depressed. That's it?"

The woman went to a desk in the corner and took an envelope from it, removed the documents, and handed them to Dane. Quigley moved in closer to read over her shoulder. He then walked over to the mother, sat next to her, held her hand, and spoke to her in a hushed tone.

Dane's disapproval abruptly came to fruition. "Whose stupid idea was it to bring us in here?" she seethed.

"This is what she wants. It's her choice," the woman feebly replied.

Dane grabbed her bag of equipment for emphasis and said, "*This* is what you do when there's no other choice. We are who you call when you don't have any other option. Your mother has plenty of options."

Dane had the poor daughter backed into a corner of the kitchen. "There's real suffering right up the street," she went on. "Depressed? What *isn't* there to be depressed about? Hell, I'm depressed. I don't remember the last time I was happy." She thrust out an arm toward Quigley and offered him a vein while still looking at the cowering woman. "Here, Quig, do me in!" Then she turned to me. "Aaron, are you happy?" She didn't wait for an answer, of course. "Maybe we should take care of Aaron, too. I haven't seen him smile all day."

The woman responded with a weak "Stop it."

Tossing the mother's medical report onto a counter,

Dane called out to Quigley, "Let's get out of here!" With my full attention on her, I had all but forgotten about him kneeling in the dark with the mother. Dane must have, too, because she was outside and halfway to the van before she realized he wasn't with us.

She turned and started back for the house. As we reached the landing, Quigley hurried out and apologized for lagging behind. The daughter stood in the open doorway. I thought I saw her mouth the words "thank you" to Quigley, and there was an abyss of dismal silence as she gave a faint, grateful smile. I could just make out her mother still sitting in the dimly lit living room.

"Quig, is everything okay?" Dane asked. "What happened?"

"I just showed her a little sympathy, that's all," Quigley replied.

Dane hesitated, taken aback by her partner's comment. Soon she was following Quigley and me with a look of growing consternation on her face. The crowd for young Bethany's funeral was thinning; people crisscrossed our path to the van.

"I'll drive," Dane said. Then, defensively, she added, "I don't condone suicide. It's just...selfish."

Dane drove and Quigley logged the call. I watched San Francisco at night through the windshield, and in the silence, I thought of my bus tour with Ben. Was there a future here, or was it doomed to be a museum, a cold display of the dead past?

Dane broke the silence. "We're not reapers, Quig. There's a difference between our job and a bunch of psychotic..." Her words trailed off as she met Quigley's obdurate gaze.

As she pulled the van onto Filbert Street, she shouted, "Oh, punch a nut!"

A pile of bodies came into view—ten or more cadavers heaped upon the sidewalk like early morning trash. As Dane called dispatch, Quigley jumped out and ran toward the mound of bodies. I followed, and when I joined him, he was leaning over a corpse that had rolled from the stack and into the street. He gently placed a hand upon the victim's shoulder. I, on the other hand, had to step back from the pungent odor and suck in some cool, damp air to avoid losing my spaghetti and meatballs from earlier that night.

"I called for a Bearer Unit," Dane told us, exiting the van, "and soldiers to secure this area. They should be here soon."

"Does this happen a lot?" I asked.

"It's not uncommon," Dane answered.

Quigley didn't move. "It's different seeing them out here, like this," he said.

"Some of them have been dead a while," Dane observed. "But they couldn't have been piled here for very long."

"How does this happen?" I asked. "Isn't this a clean area?"

"It was. Now it's contaminated," Dane explained. "They might have been laid here for exactly that reason."

"Who would do that?"

"Extremists," she said. With a glance to Quigley, she added, "Or reapers."

The neighborhood was like any other, vacant and dark (except with an overwhelming stench of death.), and there was that ever-hovering, foreboding quiet that had a way of turning all your senses up to eleven. The sudden, piercing sound of an infant's wail from a nearby apartment startled the three of us. Dane squeezed her eyes shut, as though trying to keep the cry out of her head.

"Colors?" I asked her.

"No. I just hate that sound."

"Do you ever euthanize children?"

"Sometimes. Usually they don't live long enough."

Two military trucks arrived, emerging from around a corner as though they had always been there, lurking. Like ants, orderly and with purpose, soldiers poured out of the vehicles and immediately went to work combing the area and barricading the perimeter. Dane identified herself and explained the situation to the captain. For me, the busy activity of the soldiers was a welcome distraction.

As Quigley pulled bodies from the heap and laid them out to make the Bearer Unit's job of tagging and bagging easier, Dane answered her phone. By the tension in her shoulders and the impatience of her pacing, I surmised that the call was not going to relieve the evening's growing drama, but rather, add to it, like one more body to the pile. Finally, her eyes wide and burning, she responded to the caller with, "Are you fucking kidding me?"

* * *

Entering a restricted area was not a problem for Dane and Quigley; their FCO identification was all they needed. I was another matter. If it were discovered who I was and that I was breaking regulations, I would be extradited back to Seattle that very moment. With that, Dane had me curl up behind the incinerator while she did a little flirting with the soldier at the checkpoint to distract him from further inspecting the van.

He let us through, and Dane drove as though we were a conventional ambulance speeding to save a life. Dane hadn't conveyed any actual information about the call she'd received; curses about "morons" and "idiots" and "that bitch" was all she'd shared. Quigley didn't know anything about the brothers sneaking off earlier that evening, but I did.

"Zac and Ben?" I asked her.

"Idiots!" was her reply. She checked her phone for the location of the call's origin. "They're not far," she said. "If they stay tight, this should be easy."

Then she complained about not having the right vehicle for the task. Normally, when entering that area, they used a van fortified with armor panels and steel mesh over the windows. To the residents here, an FCO van was a symbol of their imprisonment and the inevitable outcome of life on "death row." Thus, the van often became an easy target for their frustration and rage.

Entering the neighborhoods south of Market was like infiltrating a concrete fortress. The immense walls of abandoned department stores and offices buildings bordered and enclosed the unlit streets. The lack of municipal lighting was the first thing I noticed; it became that all-important ingredient for the cliché graveyard simile.

"They brought it on themselves," Dane explained about the neighborhood. "After Fades took over North Beach, it still remained a functioning part of the city. But the violence down here only made the rest of city want to forget about them. They'll all be dead here sooner than later, anyway."

"Makes you wonder what their fighting for, then," Quigley added.

"So they *won't* be forgotten?" I wondered aloud.

The street we traveled could have been anywhere in the city, really. The cement of the sidewalks, the bricks of the buildings, the asphalt beneath us were the same as everywhere else. It was the stories I'd read that had me on edge: the transit bus that was hijacked, tipped over, and set on fire with the passengers still aboard; the dumpster that was found full of bodies, each with its genitalia pulverized by a blunt instrument.

Dane drove down the middle of the street, saying it gave her room to negotiate obstacles, if needed. Considering the speed she was going, I hoped that we wouldn't have to dodge someone or something; the cumbersome van couldn't have been easy to maneuver in an emergency.

Fortunately, we made it to the school without incident. From what we could see, the vicinity was desolate of people. A playing field covered in parked cars with a chain-link fence collapsed upon some of them was a peculiar sight. Dane slowed the van but had no intention of stopping unless absolutely necessary. Quigley and I peered deeply into the shadows for the brothers while Dane kept an eye out for undesirables. She circled the parking area until the van's headlights illuminated Zac, Ben, and a woman I surmised to be Natyli, surrounded by four children in front of a dome of blankets and cardboard. Three of the children held makeshift weapons of wooden sticks and steel rods, and the fourth wielded a knife with a blade as long as his arm.

There were two boys and two girls. They appeared to be between the ages of five and eight and were haggard and wild-eyed. One pair of brother and sister would have been cute, with their freckled faces and frizzy red hair, if it hadn't been for their bloodlust grimaces. Dane rolled down her window, and the children bombarded the night with curt remarks:

"What are you doing in our house?"

"Where's our mother?"

"Don't you rape her again!"

Natyli pointed a gun at Knife Boy. It was a standoff. Zac

stood petrified, Ben tried to diplomatically reason with them, and the four hardened, vigilant children were ready to pounce. None of them noticed us, even with the van's high beams shining on them, until Dane called out. Zac reacted by fleeing toward the van before anyone else.

"Open the door!" Dane ordered me.

As I slid the side door wide, Quigley jumped from his seat and ran past Zac. Dane shouted for him to stop, but then saw what he was running toward—the children with sticks striking Ben and Natyli across their legs and arms. Quigley grabbed two of the little aggressors, one under each arm, allowing Ben and Natyli to make a break for the van. That left Quigley alone to become their personal six-foot-plus piñata.

For a moment, it was comical—Quigley nervously laughed and *mmrp*ed with every whack he received. That quickly changed, however, when Knife Boy made a move for him. With a twist, Quigley threw one child into him, tossed the other on top of both of them, and then ran in our direction, the fourth child frantically swinging her stick at him. When Quigley took a final leap into the van, the little terror stopped at the sight of us.

FCO vehicles were not marked—letters or insignia only made for clearer targets—but anyone who'd seen one knew. Our headlights glaring at her, the little girl with red hair and freckles began to scream.

"Reapers! Reapers!"

The other children joined in and came at us. They grabbed handfuls of rocks and pelted the windows of the van as they charged. In a flash, they were upon us, hitting the sides and doors with their sticks. Knife Boy was about to take his blade to one of the tires when Dane slammed into reverse. The jolt sent all of us in the back tumbling forward. Quigley's forehead knocked into the windshield.

In a maneuver that nearly tipped the van on its side, Dane spun us around and sped forward. A series of turns and we were well away from the children and the whole crazy scene. We were also far from the route we had taken to get there. Dane cursed while Quigley checked his system for a way out. He gave her a number of directions that eventually took us up a narrow street with no outlet, only a military barricade.

"This is a dead end! What the hell!" Dane exclaimed.

"It must be new," Quigley answered. "It's not in the system!"

Before Dane could let loose with another flurry of expletives, the van was showered by stones hurled from the darkness—not small rocks like the children had thrown, either, but chunks of concrete and bricks the size of softballs. Supplies were jolted from the shelves, a box of needles bounced off Zac's head, and spiderwebs of cracks spread across the windshield. Cries of "Reapers!" further punctuated the hailstorm. We couldn't tell how many assailants there were—dozens, by the number of glowing wristbands dancing about the blackness. And curiously, they were of all hues—green and orange, as well as red.

Dane backed up and turned our clumsy vehicle around as the popping of brick against metal, like gunshots, echoed upon us. We all yelled at Dane to get us out of there, and she yelled at us to shut up. The four of us in the back were jostled into each other, as Dane would alternately brake, accelerate, and swerve to avoid the silhouetted figures that assailed us.

"Part of me wanted to run them over," Dane later confessed. "And part of me couldn't blame them for wanting to harm us."

Quigley's new directions got us heading back the way we had come, all of us feeling as beat up as the van appeared. Despite Quigley's assurance that we were in the clear, Dane kept us flying along. She had no intention of slowing until we were back through the checkpoint.

And even if she hadn't been driving in such a rush, it wouldn't have mattered about the soaring beer bottle that came out of nowhere. It couldn't have been avoided.

All the factors were in place: our speed, the force of which the empty bottle was thrown, and the cracked, weakened state of the windshield. Upon impact, both bottle and window shattered—no, *disintegrated*—into a million shards with a dull but loud pop. Dane and Quigley were able to close their eyes. The rest of us covered ourselves from the shower of glass. For a moment after, the only sounds were the engine and the bluster of cold wind coming through the nonexistent windshield.

Dane slowed the van and called out to everyone, making sure we were all okay. Her face was covered with a dozen pinpricks of blood—Quigley's, too. Everyone responded that they were fine, and Dane continued to drive at a less severe pace.

"That was tense, huh?" Natyli said with a disturbing grin.

The checkpoint came into view. Dane knew it would be a bit more difficult to hide the four of us; before, it had just been me. She turned and told us, "Lie down and play dead."

"What?" Natyli questioned.

"Just do it! Don't move. Don't breath."

We approached the checkpoint; the four of us lay still and silent, like good little cadavers. Dane's fast talking was impressive. She explained to the soldier, the same one whom she had flirted with earlier, that there were no available Bearer Units and she needed to get the infected bodies to the crematorium immediately. The soldier, dumbfounded by her rapid-fire eloquence, waved us through without any comments regarding the missing windshield and blood-spotted faces of Dane and Quigley.

Just another night for the FCO, he might have thought.

SORROWFUL SONGS

It was a cold, gusty drive to Natyli and Drake's place in the Richmond District. Natyli was the only one of us who wasn't edgy from the excitement, unaffected by the precarious events of earlier; she seemed very much within her element.

I was nursing a banged-up elbow. Ben was serious, contemplative, not the lighthearted young man I had met only two days before, and Zac did his best to keep it together, wide-eyed and shaking, his chin in his hands, mouth covered. Dane and Quigley, their faces spotted with dried blood, were focused on getting us home safely.

"Take Geary instead of Balboa," Natyli calmly instructed Dane. "We can come up behind my apartment and avoid the crowd."

The crowd she referred to had to do with the Halloween parade that would soon be passing by her building; it was closing in on Golden Gate Park, where it would culminate into an orgiastic, frenzied gathering reminiscent of the

1960s—only, not the beautiful, peaceful experience I'd read about, but angry and ugly. When we stopped to let her off, Natyli invited us in to join a party she and Drake were having.

"We do this every year," she told us. "We have a bunch of people over and watch the parade of freaks from our rooftop. It goes on for hours. Come on, you all look like you could use some downtime."

We looked at each other and agreed that she was right. As the parade clamored from blocks away, we poured out of the van and followed Natyli to the rear entrance of her apartment building. She dialed her code into the intercom and waited. A moment later, a dull male voice came through the speaker, barely audible above the mélange of chatter and blaring music in the background.

"Who's there?"

"It's Natyli," she answered.

The door buzzed and we entered. Immediately, Natyli's mood changed. She ran fiercely up the three flights of stairs to her apartment. We did our best to keep up with her. By the time we made it to the third floor, she was already in her apartment, going after the unfortunate soul who had buzzed us in.

"Nobody comes in without the password!" Natyli yelled, her voice carrying into the stairwell. "Remember that? What are you doing just letting us in here?"

Through the open door, we could view Natyli standing

toe-to-toe with an older man; his dazed, droopy eyelids barely widened as the volume of her voice increased.

"Do you even remember the password?" she continued.

"Yes, I remember," he said firmly, then pulled strands of his long hair away from his unshaven face as he considered the question. "It's...'freak show.'"

"So what are you doing letting us in without the password?"

"I knew it was you."

I thought it odd that Natyli simply hadn't let herself into her own residence. Instead, she had waited outside and announced who she was without offering the password, almost as though she'd wanted to rip into someone for the sake of ripping, and the barely cognitive doorman was an easy target.

"Don't let anyone in without the password!" she reiterated.

As the rest of us stepped up to enter, the old, spacey doorman put a hand up for us to stop, obviously waiting for that all-important phrase. Zac was first.

"Uh...freak show?" he said and was allowed to pass.

One at a time, four more declarations of "freak show" followed, and soon we were all inside. The doorman, satisfied with the job he had done, proudly closed the door behind us as we melded with the forty-odd other guests.

Natyli and Drake's apartment was a renovated flat; many of the original walls had been taken out to create an open living area with easy access to the kitchen and lots of windows. In a corner was a spiral staircase leading to a door in the ceiling. Adjacent to the main room were two small bedrooms and one bathroom. It was difficult to discern a particular design style: neoclassic Asian, contemporary urban, or American bargain flea market?

Minutes later, Natyli emerged from one of the bedrooms, having changed into a dress that wasn't quite a sari and not exactly a muumuu; it was tight in all the right places and loose where it needed to be. She went directly to the stereo system, turned off the pounding bass and techno highs of the music that was playing, and replaced it with the third movement of Górecki's Third Symphony. It was a piece I knew well.

Her freshly made-up face glowed; her hair sparkled of glitter. She was an undeniably striking woman, and she was gracious to ignore my gaping at her as she approached the five of us. She acknowledged Dane and Quigley.

"Oh, you two need to clean up your faces!" she said. "The bathroom is right that way. You'll find antiseptic above the sink." Like a perfect hostess, she instructed the rest of us to relax and make her home our own. There was food, drink, and plenty of recreational "distractions."

I told her I would be happy to just sit and listen to her choice of music.

"It sets a better mood than that other crap, doesn't it?" she commented. "There's something about it that allows you to get grounded, especially after a night like tonight."

I imagined, for her, every night was "a night like tonight." She added that the previous music had been Drake's choice and indicated it wasn't the only thing upon which they disagreed. I guessed that the few select, cohesive furnishings were hers and the bargain junk was his; much of the artwork, in particular, had a stylistic stamp on it, probably Natyli's, while I'm sure the thrift store–bin prints belonged to Drake. Speaking of whom, he was nowhere to be seen.

The five of us split up, squeezing in wherever we could. Ben took a seat on a chair's armrest so he could stay close to the door and watch the whole room. Zac kept moving, fidgeting from one spot to another, sitting on the floor here or leaning against a wall there. Dane and Quigley returned, their faces cleaned and looking only slightly marred; then they went in separate directions in search of refreshments. I found a vacant spot on the couch tucked between a couple who reeked of incense.

A new piece of music began—this one rich with strings and woodwinds. As the layered melody settled upon the room like a warm mist, so was the atmosphere significantly altered: a room that had once been energized by people shouting above a thunder of drums and power chords now gelled into an earnest, brooding space, one that invited intimacy (another example of the dichotomy that defined Natyli and Drake's relationship). After that came the sublime piano of Rachmaninoff.

I wanted to speak with Ben about his father's three wishes, but he was distracted, constantly scanning the room and watching the front door. I knew I was flying out of the city later that day, though, so I made a move to talk with him, distracted or not.

"How do you know Natyli?" A smooth, lilting voice interrupted my plan.

I turned to see a girl in her late teens with almond eyes and skin like polished teak. While there was something in her eyes, something to which I wanted to respond, I couldn't answer her right away—I was stopped by the fact that a good part of her face was missing. From the left side of her upper lip, through her nose, to between her eyes was a canal of scar tissue, as though someone had intended to cut her head in half, but failed, leaving a badly healed crevice.

As I looked away and stuttered, I saw on the other side of her a long, thin, dark-skinned young man with no discernible muscle tone whose face was covered in burn scars. Their deliberate pattern of symmetry hinted that they were self-inflicted. I realized I was sitting next to Mutts, like those Ben had mentioned in his journal. ("They deliberately disfigure themselves with burns or cuts," he had written.) Exactly why they practiced self-mutilation was unclear.

"I don't really know her," I eventually said. "I'm here with some friends of hers."

"She has friends?" the young man replied.

I laughed and shrugged. "I've only just met her."

"I'm Shel," said the young man. "This is Lucy."

"My name is Aaron."

"Honestly, Aaron," Lucy said, "except for the tall one with the dreads, none of you looks like you would know Natyli or Drake. What's your story?"

"Lucy likes a good story," Shel interjected.

"I don't know how good a story it is," I began clumsily.

Lucy slid from the couch and sat on the floor; she rested her head upon a cushion and a hand upon my knee, truly ready and intent upon hearing an interesting account of how the five of us had come to be in Natyli's apartment. As best and colorfully as I could, I explained the circumstances of my being there in the city and what had transpired that night. Although others around us leaned in for a better listen, I saw the true success of my narrative in Lucy's face. Her smile dissolved the sobering dissonance of one of Bartok's string quartets playing in the background; her glow soon masked her deformity.

I also had Ben's attention. "That isn't the half of what happened," he added when I was done. From there, we all listened as he related, with great detail, everything that had occurred to him and Zac that night at The Fallout. He was a natural and bursting to share his experience with someone— in this case, a rapt audience of about fifteen people. For a good thirty minutes, like a charismatic preacher, Ben's passionate eloquence kept us mesmerized.

"I've seen them before," Lucy said at one point, "those guys with the pointed hair and leather jackets. You're lucky. They ruin people hard."

Zac, who had been slowly pacing behind us, asked, "Where? Where have you seen them?" He eyes were wild, as though he expected them to be right behind him.

Lucy paused thoughtfully before answering. "Not anywhere around here. Don't worry."

Zac wandered off, not at all relieved. I wondered what could have occurred for lovely, damaged Lucy to cross paths with the pointy-haired goons. Maybe she wasn't a Mutt, but rather, *they* had done that to her face. Her injury did resemble Ben's description of the woman in the jungle gym. Could their situations have been similar? Had the same gang "ruined" both of them?

"Is he your brother?" Lucy asked Ben, who nodded. "I can see a resemblance."

"Only slight," said Shel.

"I think he's cute," she added.

"He looks nervous," Shel commented.

"He's got a lot on his mind," Ben said.

"No. I wouldn't say that. I think he's just very nervous."

"You're right," Ben said with a grin. "He doesn't have much of anything on his mind."

Behind Ben, Dane stood, a cup of warm drink in her hand. She, too, had heard Ben's account of The Fallout. I couldn't begin to guess what was on her mind: the suicidal mother, Quigley's behavior, Zac and Drake and Natyli and their games. She melted into the party, as though to avoid the rest of us.

Ben expressed concern about his mother, stating that he shouldn't have gone out that night, and suggested we all start heading home. "But then," he said, "it's three in the morning, and she's probably asleep."

"If you hadn't come here, we wouldn't have met you," Lucy was telling Ben, "and we wouldn't have heard a great story."

I reminded Ben of what Nikki had said: his mother wasn't stupid; she knew of the post-curfew outings.

"It doesn't keep her from worrying," Ben responded. "And we're not usually out this late."

People coming through the front door (each announcing the obligatory "freak show") then distracted him, and I turned to Lucy.

"I'd like to hear a story now," I told her. "I'd like to know what happened to you."

She gave a sad smile and said, "That's not a good story."

Shel took my shoulder. "Have you been up to the roof yet? Come on."

He led me to the spiral staircase in the corner of the room. Once reaching the top stair, you had to heft yourself upward through a cramped crawl space in the ceiling and flip aside a door to the tarred surface of the roof. It was obvious that access to the rooftop was a feature exclusive to that apartment, added either by Drake and Natyli or previous tenants.

The rooftop was a welcomed retreat, a safe harbor from the city. Though only three stories up, there was a comforting disconnection from the goings-on below and beyond. At least another twenty people were up there, talking, laughing, and huddling beneath the cold wind that was clearing the sky of clouds and fog in preparation for the coming dawn.

Shel took me to the edge, and we looked down on the street. The Halloween parade, having started weeks before and growing with every city block it crawled along, was beginning to fill the neighborhood. From the rooftop, as safe a vantage point as one could have, the parade had a hypnotic attraction: there were sequined dancers weaving around goblins, zombies, and grim reapers; the colorful costumes, streamers, and ribbons all moved along with an ocean-like rhythm. It didn't take long, however, before the festival's purpose became apparent—embracing the horrible to survive the reality.

Marchers below threw objects at us. We dodged garbage, stones, and shoes flung our way as we peered downward. Before the holiday's end, even with police patrols, many an innocent bystander would be accosted and forced to march; the more they resisted, the more they were assaulted, and women were often raped.

I caught sight of two naked young girls completely

painted as skeletons running through the crowd, shoving people aside as they went. They came upon a man wearing an absurdly oversize rubber mask in the likeness of our president. The skeletal nymphs turned the mask into their personal punching bag and proceeded to slap and hit away, disregarding the human being underneath. The man stumbled and fell. The girls punched until the mask came off his blood-soaked head. After laughing wildly and kicking at the now lone mask a few times, they melded with the throng, leaving the bleeding man to trip off in a daze and eventually vanish around a corner. Shel and I knew it would have been pointless and self-destructive to try to help him.

We had seen enough and turned our backs to the parade. We took in the more peaceful side of the neighborhood as the sounds of demented gaiety droned behind us. I apologized to Shel for upsetting Lucy.

"Don't worry about it," he replied. "She doesn't mind people knowing about the accident; she just doesn't like to talk about it."

"Accident? I thought it was a choice—you know, self-inflicted."

"Well, let's say it was unintentional. Not like *this*." He pointed to the scars on his face.

"Why did you do that?" I asked.

"To empathize, to connect, with the pain of others. How can we really enjoy our lives knowing there is so much suffering everywhere?"

"You're protesting?"

"We're embracing."

A philosophy not unlike those marching below, I thought. Then I asked, "What happened to Lucy?"

"She tried to kill herself," Shel explained. "Back when you could still buy a pistol from down the street. But, well, she missed. She says her finger slipped on the trigger before she was ready."

The image of a bullet ripping open the front of her face was somehow more gruesome than if she had actually succeeded in spraying parts of her brain onto a wall.

"I told her that she missed because she really didn't want to die," Shel continued, "and I thank her every day for missing, because I cherish her being in my life."

"Why did she want to die?" I asked, realizing it was somehow a stupid question. Hadn't I seen enough reasons in my time there?

Shel then told me about Lucy being kidnapped by Fades, then drugged to the point of incoherency, but just lively enough that she could be rented out for sex. It was a common, horrifying occurrence, he explained. "Lucy says there are dozens of them—girls and boys younger than her, women and men, all imprisoned within a motel on the wharf. Those who aren't lucky enough to die are eventually released as diseased drug addicts."

"Did she go to the authorities?"

"Yes, but no one wants to believe her. Maybe they're

afraid of starting a riot, or they fear the restricted areas. Maybe they just don't care. Who knows? It's no secret that that part of town has been forgotten."

"What happened to Lucy? How did she get out?"

"That's the good part of the story, the inspiring part. She fought her way out, man. She got the hell away from there by sheer aggression and raw determination."

I couldn't imagine small, wispy Lucy with the chocolate voice being as tough as a marine. Shel must've picked up on what I was thinking, because he said, "I know. It's hard to believe. But she's a fighter."

"Yes, but..." I said, forming my hand into the shape of a gun and putting it in my mouth.

"She gave up on waiting for things to get better."

"She wanted to escape," I said. It was a common desire—to get away. Peter had it for his mother. Nikki had it. The jungle gym–dwelling mother had it.

"No, Lucy doesn't want to leave. She loves it here. We both do," Shel said. "I had to remind her that it can't be like this forever. So now we wait together."

He was right. It would be wonderful to witness this city's resurrection. Lucy and Shel's thinking was more aligned with that of Mrs. Elliot's. "We don't intend to leave. This is our home," she had said. And though Lucy had had a moment of weakness, I believed in her. And in Shel. Someday the plague would take enough lives. Walking a few city blocks would not illicit desperate fear. Families wouldn't live in abandoned cages. The fog of sorrow would clear. *That* was what I had seen in the eyes of the girl with the torn face—not hope, but more. In Lucy, I saw the *expectation* of something better.

I wondered about Dane. With which opinion did her thoughts align? She never spoke of wanting to escape. And she didn't talk about her expectations for the future. She only lamented that "this had to happen to such a beautiful city." Perhaps Dane's chosen method of coping was to live day to day, never looking to the past or tomorrow. But was that healthy? Or was it as destructive as putting a gun in your mouth?

*   *   *

Voices came up through the roof's crawl space, sounds of a confrontation. Shel and I hurried back down into the apartment, where Natyli and Drake were embroiled in a shouting match. Zac and Ben were in close proximity, looking to contribute something to the quarrel. The argument was about how Drake had left them stranded outside The Fallout. I then realized it was Drake whom Ben had been watching for.

The couple went at each other like a pair of small dogs. Yet, at the same time, Drake was smiling, and there was a twinkle in Natyli's narrowed eyes, like it was a kind of foreplay between them. The other guests showed little concern to the intensity of the yelling. It was as though they had seen it before, and Zac and Ben gave up trying to have their say. The spat ended with Natyli punching Drake's chest, pushing him into a door, and walking away, all of which he took with a laugh.

While we were on the roof, partygoers had begun bombing and passing out POGO sticks. The apartment was filled with smoke and pungent, sweet hemp aromas. It only took a minute for me to feel dizzy from the lingering haze. I found Dane against a wall, sitting cross-legged on a collection of cushions and looking as though she had inhaled via a more direct method. Her head rested in one hand; the other rubbed her eyes.

"I could've done something more for her," she mumbled.

"Done what for whom?" I asked.

"That depressed woman, Diana. I should have helped her."

"What would you have done?"

"I don't know. Something." Dane rubbed her eyes again and groaned.

Slow, lilting orchestral strings filled my brain like smoke filled the room. My eyes widened in an attempt to actually see the notes and chords floating about. Through the fog, Natyli came toward me, saying something about bologna and asiago. I was puzzled, wondering what lunch meat and cheese had to with anything.

"What?" I asked her.

She knelt close to me and repeated, "The music, it's

Albinoni's Adagio in G minor. You looked like you were enjoying it."

"It's beautiful."

"Yes, it is. I think listening to this music must be what praying feels like, but better." She placed a hand upon my leg and squeezed it as she stood. Her silky, flowing dress seemed to change colors with the adagio's melodious tones. For a moment, I thought I might be experiencing Dane's condition of synaesthesia.

Natyli made it a point to tell me about other pieces of music she played that night. A couple I recognized: Pachelbel's Canon and another adagio, one by Samuel Barber. Every piece was haunting and reverent—each, as she put it, like a prayer.

Dane curled up on the cushions and closed her eyes. I searched for Ben. My head pounding, I wanted to talk to him while I could still focus my thoughts. Fortunately, he came over and sat with us.

"How's she doing?" he asked, gently pressing a hand to Dane's hair. "She's been hitting it pretty hard since we got here."

"I think she's approaching the runway, ready to take off," I said.

"I can hear you," she responded. Her eyes closed, she reached a drowsy hand up to take Ben's. "I haven't departed yet. I'm fine."

Ben finally seemed comfortable and relaxed, so I said to

him, "I read your journals."

He didn't answer, perhaps distracted by Dane's hand upon his. He waited for me to continue.

"The entry about you visiting the zoo with your father was especially interesting," I said.

"Which one?" he asked. "There's more than one. I went there a couple of times with him. I guess you didn't read everything."

"There's a lot to read," I replied.

"Yes, writing all that stuff has been therapeutic for me. I guess I've needed a lot of therapy."

"I read the one about the three wishes. What's the other one?"

"My dad and I snuck into the zoo one night."

"You won't be able to do that anymore," interrupted Drake. Behind him stood his friend Easter, as stoic as I remember him. They had been mingling and heard our conversation. I looked at Drake as he stood over us, striking his best pose. But as hard as he tried, Drake was anything but formidable; he had a presence that oozed of childish annoyance much more than machismo and intimidation. "They found the hole and plugged it up yesterday," he went on. "There's no way to sneak in now."

Drake slid a chair close to me and sat. "You live in the Northwest, right?"

"Yes. Seattle," I replied.

"What's it like there? Is it bad?"

His question caught the interest of much of the room; people gathered around. Shel took a place behind me, and Lucy sat on the floor in front, awaiting another story.

"It was bad at first," I said. "No rioting, but a lot of deaths and general panic. We had a better idea of what was happening because it had already happened here. If it hadn't been for the quarantine, it would have been a lot worse; half the country might have been wiped out."

"You're welcome," Drake said.

Some sardonic laughs from others around the room accented his opinion.

"I can only imagine how difficult it's been. But what else could have been done?"

"It's not about what was done, man," said a voice through the smoke. "It's about what's happening *now*. We're prisoners here! Like we're being punished!"

"The quarantine had its place, but now it's unnecessary," said someone from the back of the room. "The infection rate has dropped significantly in recent months. Now only a few neighborhoods should be quarantined. The rest of us should be allowed to get back to our lives."

"And the curfew is ridiculous! Like we're prisoners! That's what you should write about, man."

From my vantage point on the floor and with the blue-gray cloud hovering just over my head, I found it difficult to hone in on whoever was speaking; they were faceless voices bouncing down at me from the ceiling and ricocheting off the walls, each with a sad story to tell.

"When I was finally able to leave the city," one woman said (I thought it was a woman), "I was so stigmatized everywhere I went that I had to come back. And I was only allowed to do that because my mother was here and dying."

Two others admitted to similar persecutions. They had planned to attend university once permitted to travel, but their applications were rejected because of the "endangerment to students, faculty, and staff." One of them was intending to take the case to the Supreme Court.

"What a waste of time that will be!" another person spouted. "The government doesn't care! Look at how they've forgotten about us here. They're just waiting for us to die so they can clean it all up and make a fortune off the real estate!"

"One big conspiracy, is it?" I commented, a bit impatiently because my brain was throbbing.

Someone else said that they weren't even from San Francisco, that they had been here visiting friends when the quarantine was enacted.

"Why the hell would you visit a place that was infested with plague?" another jeered.

This spawned a debate about the source of the plague and why it hadn't been eradicated. More conspiracy theories came out. Soon everyone was talking over one other.

I slid from my cushion on the floor and laid my heavy head back upon Dane's knees. I looked up to see Zac appear beside Drake. By their gestures and expressions, Zac was angry, and Drake thought it was funny. The angrier Zac became, the funnier it was to Drake. It was difficult to make out what they were saying, but I did catch "We could've been killed!" and "Your games are getting way too dangerous!" from Zac, and Drake responded with something like, "Of course, that's what it's all about!" and lots of laughing.

"Sometimes you don't even know you're in the middle of a game," Drake then said. "Like when the three of you went to that showing, or whatever it was, and it was raided by Cross Hunters. Remember that? It was me and some others, you gumps! And you never figured it out! God hates cowards! Remember?" Drake screamed with laughter.

Ben had overheard. Both brothers were transported back to whenever that night was; it was evident in their faces. Dane, too, reacted by lifting her head with a wide-eyed look at Drake.

"Ain't that a punch in the nuts?" grunted Easter. (So he could speak, after all!)

"Did you really believe that shit was real?" Drake added.

When I recalled what happened next, it was in slow motion. But in reality, it was instantaneous. Ben lunged for Drake! As I said, Ben was strong for his size, and he took Drake down like a linebacker tackling a scarecrow. Before he knew it, Drake was on the floor beneath a flurry of misdirected punches.

Zac stepped in, but one of Ben's flailing blows caught

him on the chin and knocked him off-balance into the shouting onlookers. Drake could do little to defend himself but cover his face and call out in a shrill pitch, "Get off me! Get him off me!" It was Dane who was able to get on top of Ben, wrap her arms around his midsection from behind, heave him off, and put him to the floor with a move resembling a wrestler's takedown.

I found myself standing, yet unable to move. Lucy helped Dane calm Ben, and Shel stepped in between them and Drake's friends. There was a cacophony of hollering, threats, and a great deal of posturing. The noise and tension was stifling.

Suddenly, two gunshots rang out! And the room fell silent.

Natyli stood on a chair, above all of us, holding her handgun high above her head. Shards of ceiling and sheetrock dust floated down upon her. It was quite dramatic, which had been her intention. My first thought was for those partygoers on the rooftop; I was expecting to hear cries come from overhead that someone had been hit. But there wasn't a sound from the roof or anywhere in the apartment. No one said anything. Natyli had made her point.

She stepped down from the chair and walked over to the stereo. Next on her playlist were the more contemporary, synthesized sounds of St. Succubus, Tangerine Dream, and Van Gogh's Ear, as meditative as the classics played earlier, yet from another era.

Ben's breathing was strained and his face red. I suggested we all go up to the roof for air. Zac led the way as he massaged his chin. Lucy and Shel followed Dane, Ben, and me up the narrow staircase. Under Natyli's baneful glare, Drake and his friends left us alone.

Those on the rooftop hardly took notice as the six of us appeared through the trapdoor, shrouded by smoke wafting upward from below. We left the door flipped open, and the hole puffed like a chimney. I, for one, felt immensely better in the cold morning air. Ben's color returned to a more natural hue. All of us relaxed in the calming hours before dawn as we huddled in a circle for warmth.

"Ben," I asked him pointedly, "what the hell was that all about?"

He laughed, embarrassed. Then, a bit agitated, he replied, "So you didn't read *that* part, either, the part about the showing?"

"No," I said.

With a sigh, Ben proceeded to tell me—tell all of us— about that night, the one so sensitive to Zac, Dane, and him.

What follows is the journal entry I hadn't read.

A SHOWING

Zac was in one of his restless moods. It was after curfew, but he wanted to go out anyway. Normally, we would be out with Dad, but he'd told us to stay in that night. He said he had to do something we couldn't be a part of. That made Zac want to go out more. My brother never liked that something might happen without him, like his life would be less if he didn't experience whatever he could. He and Drake are always trying to make something happen for themselves. But I don't think it really counts if your experiences are so made up.

Zac told us he wanted to go out, go anywhere, and Dane asked him where he wanted to go. As always, he just wanted to go for a walk. Like always, he said, "You don't have to go with me if you don't want to," as though it were some kind of challenge. And, of course, we went out with him because we wanted to be out there as much as he did.

There was still a lot of garbage from the last riot lining the streets. I caught the smell of cooking grease from a nearby café, one of the few remaining in the city. We didn't have to walk very far before we found something happening. There was a collage of sounds like music and conversation not far from us. It was hard to tell one element from another as it bounced around the empty neighborhood. But Zac said he knew the direction it was coming from, so Dane and I followed.

We began to see other people. They seemed afraid of us, or at least cautious, and Dane thought it was a good idea for us to do the same, so we kept an appropriate distance. It got hard to do that, though, because we were all heading toward the same sounds. We were like rats to a piper. Many people stayed in the shadows, and some, like the three of us, walked the center of the street.

A gust of wind threw a flurry of papers at our feet. One, a red flyer, stuck to my leg. I pulled it off and looked at the image drawn upon it, a sketching with bold lines of a straw dog, often a symbol of sacrifice. I let the flyer go, and it fluttered away down the street.

Dane took Zac's hand and asked him again where we were going. He didn't answer right away. We made it to a corner from around which we had seen a warm yellow-orange glow. There in the middle of the street was a bonfire and a crowd in front of a condemned neighborhood community center. Zac pointed and said, "There!"

Dozens of people were spread out everywhere, some around the fire and some by the building. The heat from the fire was intense. I stayed back, but Zac and Dane went closer. They stood there a minute and absorbed the glow. There were a few smaller fires about the area and more inside the community center. Smoke was rising into the night sky from holes in the roof. Nearly all the windows above were shattered, and the music we heard earlier trickled over the rotting sills and panes to the crowd gathering below. The music was sad and dull; it sounded like a violin that was underwater with a pulsing, offbeat rhythm.

I noticed two things: hundreds of red flyers like the one that had stuck to my leg dotted the ground like drops of blood marking a trail, and our dad's truck was parked on the street just past the building. I told Zac, and he decided that we had to go inside.

People were gathered around the entrance beneath a shredded green awning, but few were entering. It was like some kind of exclusive club.

"What's going on?" Dane asked quietly.

Some others around answered her with, "A showing."

Then I asked the obvious question. "What's a showing?"

A small woman stepped from behind me. The left half of her head was shaved bald, and in place of her hair was a long, wide scar, jagged like a lightning bolt, with a tattooed outline that jutted down the back of her neck. It was the first time I had ever seen a Mutt. The scarring was so gross that I hoped it would be the last.

"It will show you things," she said, "things that have happened and things that are going to happen." Her voice had a faraway sound.

Where the people were mingling around the entrance there was an old man standing, partly cloaked in the shadow of a dark canvas curtain that served as a door. His thin, pale arm seemed to glow as it stretched out from the doorway, selecting individuals to enter. The chosen would step forward and slink through the parted canvas. I think he was going to choose everyone eventually but did it randomly to make it seem more mysterious.

We were there only a moment before the old man picked the three of us out of the crowd. It was creepy to see that finger of translucent skin and bone point right at me, and then watching the skeletal hand unfold and wave us in gave me a chill. Zac pulled Dane forward, cutting through the people, and Dane grabbed my hand and ahead we went.

The black canvas opened for us like the slit of a cat's eye as we stepped into a large octagonal room with the light of a thousand candles and the heat of a hundred bodies. It looked to me as though the building's interior had been gutted and all of its walls replaced with those canvas drapes. The surrounding candles stretched our shadows upward like fingers reaching for holes in the ceiling.

The three of us slowly moved forward with the group. Every few steps, I got a better view of what was ahead of us. We were funneling through one wall of the octagon that *led to another room. But first, each person had to submit to a ceremonial wash, a cleansing. There were three bath-size steel tubs with intricate floral patterns painted on their sides. In between those were small black cauldrons sitting upon ornate pedestals. There was a choice of just how "cleansed" we wanted to be.*

The majority of individuals used the cauldrons to wash their faces and hands. Many made it a ritual by pausing with the water cupped in their hands before pressing it to their faces, not splashing. Then they would lean back and allow the fluid to run down their necks, chests, and arms.

A few would disrobe and step into the tubs. Attendants, who were barely clothed themselves, would ladle water over the bathers and hand out towels to those who wanted them. Some dried off, while others didn't. Still others didn't even bother to collect their clothes before running away to the next room.

As it became our turn, I grew anxious at the idea of Dane getting undressed and soaking herself in one of the tubs. But she didn't. Not because she was shy, but because, like she later told me, "Who knows how many have washed off their skank in that water?"

She was right. The water in the cauldrons was being replenished, but not in the tubs. The three of us chose to experience only the cool facial wash. I don't know how purifying it was, but it was definitely refreshing in the room's muggy heat. Zac let go with a vigorous "Whoop!"

We walked ahead to the next room. It was a maze of canvas walls that billowed and waved with the motion of people scuttling through. As we shuffled along slowly, others ran past in either direction, either lost or playing. There were the sounds of giggling and laughing all around. And music. Ahead of me, Dane began to sway with the rhythm. With a rare smile, she invited me to join her. I couldn't resist.

Zac was ahead of us in a sort of meditative haze. He seemed to no longer care where he was going or whether Dane and I followed. Past another curtain and we were in the biggest room yet. Off from it were other areas where people congregated. In a corner of the central room were musicians surrounded by dancers. We were pulled in to join them. It was easy to fall in sync with the group because of the hypnotic rhythm. My brother and Dane were smiling and twirling about each other.

I fell away from the crowd to find myself facing a nude woman holding a decorative goblet. She wanted me to drink. I ignored its pungent odor and took a swallow. The sickly-sweet syrup coated my tongue and throat. The woman threw her head back and laughed. The face I made amused her. I asked her what it was, and she told me it was "truth."

That truth, as the naked woman called it, took effect quickly. My head became flushed and numb. My whole body felt heavy. I began looking for a place to sit.

Instead, I found my father. He stood with dozens of people sitting around him on a pillow-covered floor. I thought I was hallucinating, because he didn't see me and I couldn't seem to form the words to speak to him. There were a lot of pastel colors and paisley patterns floating about in the area. I sat and fell over into others who were behind me. Someone propped me up, and I closed my eyes and listened to my father's words. I was in a kind of dreamlike state as I listened to his "Would God exist without religion?" sermon.

Whatever I drank wore off as quickly as it had come. I snapped out of my haze to hear my father arguing with some of those around him. They weren't sitting at his feet anymore, but standing and closing in on him. He fervently told them how he had never supported their cause and how they had gotten his message all wrong. He was especially confronting a skinny, tall man, taller than anyone else in the room, who wore glasses that made him look like a giant bug.

"There is nothing original in hating humankind. You're not the first," my father said to him. "We are a disgusting species and a disappointment to God. But you're no better. What you've done is not for you to decide. You are not soldiers nor shepherds, but just one more of God's disappointments!"

I couldn't quite make out the rest of what my father said, but I think he said something about going to the police, which caused an uproar from those around him. Some of them pushed at my father. I shouted to him, but my voice was lost to the deafening noise. I shoved and plowed through the crowd until I reached him.

I put my arms around him, and he shouted, "What are you doing here? You shouldn't be here!"

"I'm here with Zac and Dane!" I told him.

He looked around for them and said, "You need to get out of here! The three of you need to go!" With a hand around my shoulder, my father pushed the two of us through the throng of people until we eventually broke free from the crowd. "Let's find your brother and get out of here!" he shouted. He seemed oblivious to the angry mob around him.

Then things got really bad. There was suddenly noise greater than what was already happening—screaming, shouting, and the popping of fireworks (or gunfire?)! More than once, I heard someone call out that it was Cross Hunters. I saw Dane and my brother standing within the eye of a cyclone of panic. My father saw them, too, and took me over to them. He yelled at my brother for the three of us to get the hell out of there, and then it was as though the crowd swept our father away in its current. Or maybe someone grabbed him. I couldn't tell. He was just gone, leaving me and Zac and Dane standing there.

The popping and flashing of firecrackers and rockets were all around. Dane took my arm. Zac was frozen, looking up. Then I saw them, too—ten or more figures in black descending from a hole in the roof. They repelled down ropes into the main room.

That was when Dane was pushed into me, and together, we went to the dusty floor. I inhaled a cloud of dirt and stood. I was coughing but able to take Dane's hand and pull her up with me. I turned to make a break for it but slammed into one of the dark-clad forms. It was like hitting a wall. I went to the ground. The figure came at me and then, just inches from my face, leapt back. He bounced and taunted me. He thrust forward, and I went to throw a punch when he jumped away again.

"What the hell! It's a dummy!" I heard Dane shout.

My tormentor was a heavy-weighted mannequin, bouncing from the end of a bungee cord. I watched it recoil and settle into a smooth swing and realized it was nothing more than a lifeless, life-size puppet. It still had an arrogant quality in the way it dangled there, and it made me fume. I kicked at its hard form until Dane grabbed me.

She pulled me to the floor and, with an anxious laugh, shouted for me to stop. There was craziness all around us. I calmed down, and Dane pointed out the real-life figures in black inciting the crowd. I saw three of them as they whooped and hollered and pushed people. One of them yelled, "Don't run! Where's everybody going? The writing's on the wall! God hates cowards!"

Their faces were covered with black masks, and a mesh concealed their eyes. They looked soulless. One came at us as Dane and I got to our feet. I put myself between her and the dark form that towered over us. I flinched when he thrust a fist forward, but he didn't hit me. He stood there and laughed.

In the chaos, many of the candles were knocked over. Who knows what took to the flames faster—the canvas curtains draped everywhere or the rotted structure they covered. Dane and I went to our hands and knees as thick smoke engulfed the space above us. People collapsed in hacking, coughing fits while we crawled for the nearest exit. "Don't stand up! Stay down!" Dane called out to everyone we scooted past.

Flames rapidly swallowed everything, and the heat made it difficult to open your eyes. In a blur, I saw my father entangled with three other men—the giant Bug Man in particular. He grabbed at my father, and they struggled.

Though the crowd was thinning, there were still a frenzied few circling about, tripping over us. Dane took a knee in her rib cage. She tumbled and twisted and rolled over, gasping for air, only to take in dust and smoke.

I could see where a hole had burned into the wall a few feet from us. Wrapping my arms around Dane, I lifted her to her feet and then plunged the two of us through the hole. The rotted, burnt wood around the opening gave little resistance against our weight. We rolled a few feet, my arms still tight around her.

I pulled Dane up and away from the flaming structure

as it began to weaken and collapse in on itself. I watched as people rushed from the building. Dane began to get her breath back, and she used the end of her shirt to wipe away smoke-filled tears. With a damp hand, she took my arm.

"Where's Zac?" she asked.

What had happened to him? And who were those men fighting with my father? The panicked crowd running past us was a jumble of bodies and faces. It was difficult to distinguish one person from the next. Then I saw five masked men in black breaking from the crowd and running down the street. They trailed high-pitched, hysterical laughter behind them. I wanted to chase them. I wanted to inflict violence like I had never wanted to before.

There were sirens in the distance but no sign of my dad or my brother. Were they still trapped inside? It was then that Zac appeared, running toward Dane and me, a look of panic on his face.

Dane said, "There he is." But it didn't sound like she was happy to see him. She blasted into a run directly at him. "You asshole! You fucking asshole!" she screamed at him.

Zac stopped short and stumbled backward beneath her flurry of slaps and punches. I hurried to pull her off him and shouted that we had to get out of there. A siren's blare and the flash of red-and-yellow lights convinced them of the urgency to leave. We ran in the opposite direction of the approaching fire, police, and military vehicles.

"Where's Dad?" Zac called out.

"He's still in there!"

"No. No, he's not! He got out!" Zac shook his head as though he were shaking off the truth.

I looked back over my shoulder as I ran. There was little left of the building, only flames and smoke.

"Come on, Ben," Zac urged, unconvincingly. "He'll be at home."

"I don't know. I don't know," I said, out of breath.

But I did know. I knew he hadn't made it out. Zac knew, too, but he wouldn't say. He won't say.

We turned up the first street we came to and didn't slow until we were sure we weren't followed. Dane was fuming, and Zac looked nauseated.

"You pushed me down, Zac!" she snapped. "You shoved me out of the way to save yourself! If it hadn't been for Ben, I'd still be in there!"

Zac apologized and kept apologizing, saying that it was an accident and that he didn't mean it, and on and on. Dane told him to stay away from her. That was how it ended between them. Zac couldn't say anything in his defense. It was over, and he knew it. There was no consoling Dane. Apparently, God and my father weren't the only ones who hated cowards.

*   *   *

Zac and Dane both had been in denial about Samuel's death. Zac especially. Ben had tried to get him to admit it, but his brother didn't want to believe that his father was buried beneath the muddy, ashen mound resting only blocks from their house.

"Why didn't you tell the Feds?" I asked Ben.

"Mom doesn't want them to dig him up," he answered. "And they would—for evidence. That's why I moved his truck someplace it wouldn't be noticed. I wanted it to look like he left, went into hiding, or whatever. Mom wants his name cleared before she tells the truth."

"So she knows, too."

"Yes, I told her. She goes by his grave every morning on her walk."

Zac couldn't speak as he fought with the truth. Dane wiped away tears with one hand and reached out to Ben with the other. The rest of us lowered our heads.

"You said there were two entries about the zoo," I eventually said to Ben. "What was the other?"

"I was with my father the night he sprayed his messages," Ben said.

Zac reacted with injured surprise. Even though he was older, it was Ben's greater maturity that warranted him the privileges and responsibilities a parent reserves for elder children. Samuel had had a different relationship, a closer bond, with Ben than he'd had with Zac. It was to Ben, I thought, whom Samuel would have most likely passed his ministry.

"That was the same night he poisoned the animals?" I

clarified.

"Our father never poisoned those animals," Ben replied with reserved impatience. "No one ever understood what he was trying to do."

"You have to admit," I said, choosing my words, "his actions have been a bit ambiguous."

"I suppose so," Ben agreed after a moment.

It was Dane who told me Samuel had laid the poison. But she had heard it from someone else, she admitted, as part of what was becoming Samuel's legend, lore born from the rampant fire of rumor and hearsay. Dane put her arms around Ben.

"I'm so sorry," she told him. "I loved him very much. You know that, don't you?"

"I know," replied Ben, his face buried in her shoulder.

They held each other for a time. Shel and Lucy were an empathetic audience. Zac looked away, unconnected, until Dane released her embrace.

"I'm cold. I need to lie down," she said and began making her way to the trapdoor, until Zac stopped her.

"Remember that gang that broke into the zoo and let the animals out of their cages?" he asked.

"Yes," she answered.

"Remember how a lot of the animals just cowered in the shadows instead of running away?"

"I remember, Zac. It was a mess."

"I never wanted to be like that."

"Like what?"

"Like those dumb, scared animals."

As she descended into the apartment, Dane sharply replied, "But that's exactly what you've always been, Zac."

I'm sure Dane knew as well as the rest of us that Zac was trying to apologize: for being afraid, for playing games, for pushing her out of his way at the showing, for not being his father, and for not being Ben. She knew it and didn't care.

The rest of us agreed it was cold out and followed Dane.

Ben paused beside his brother. "You're not like that," he told him. "She's just upset."

While much of the smoke had cleared, the air in the apartment was still warm and heavy. Some girls were in the middle of the room playing and posing with Natyli's gun. It was almost as disconcerting to witness their false sense of power as it was watching them play with a loaded weapon. Dane especially was not happy.

"Natyli!" she yelled, with a gesture toward the girls. "What the hell?"

Natyli stepped in and took the gun. "We can't have any of that, now, can we?" she said. Then, popping out the clip of ammo, she handed it back to them. "Never play with a loaded gun."

Dane wasn't satisfied. She snatched the pistol from a young girl with green hair, who then berated Dane for butting in. "Get shredded!" Dane replied as she tucked the gun into the waistband of her jeans. The girl and her friends sulked off to the roof.

Dane found herself a set of cushions in a far corner of the room and curled upon them in a snug fetal position. The rest of us gathered around her, sitting or lying wherever. Faint, barely discernible music crept slowly across the floor. Its circular, breathing melody gradually, effortlessly grew louder, like an ocean tide, wave by wave, growing upon a shore. It was Górecki's Third Symphony again, this time from the beginning.

Written in 1976 (long before anyone in the room or their parents were born), the work was comprised of three movements, or "songs." The first was set to a lament from a fifteenth-century monastery; the second, a prayer found upon the wall of a Gestapo cell by an imprisoned eighteen-year-old girl; and the third, a folk song of Poland, one in which a mother mourned the death of her son.

"I don't hear grief as much as I do bittersweet celebration," Natyli commented as we listened. "Celebration of lives lived." She was sitting with Quigley, discussing society's "expendables" and how so many people existed without the slightest hint of purpose.

Natyli's idea of celebration was deviant, to say the least, I thought. The symphony was a grieving, mournful piece that confronted and encompassed immeasurable suffering. At once too painful to hear and too beautiful to ignore, the music washed over the room—wretched, ascetic spirituality dripping from every note. I listened as though it were for the first time; I listened in the same way that I knew death and sorrow were inevitabilities to someday be faced, ones that we were all presently facing. I was impelled to listen. And I wasn't alone.

I could see Dane felt it, too, bathing in it. Her eyes were closed. Her head moved with a slow sway, as though it were adrift, separate from her body. Her brow tensed, questioning, straining to hear, to see, to understand. Her breathing became irregular as the ethereal vocals of the soprano filled her senses. She saw *something*, and it seemed to terrify yet lure her. Her eyes still shut, Dane reached a hand upward to touch it, to feel it. I longed to know what was in her head at that moment.

Then the soprano's voice swelled to its visceral crescendo. It crested, and as the orchestra's strings came back with their powerful, spiral melody—

Dane's eyes opened. She gasped, resuscitated from a deep, passionate trance, and a single cathartic tear emerged from the corner of her eye. She sat up. She went to Quigley and grabbed him by the collar.

"We have to go," she said, pulling him up.

She gathered the brothers and me. Shel and Lucy followed. It was time to go. Dane had a mission.

MARTYRS OF DOOM

Six a.m. was approaching; in about thirty minutes, the curfew would be over. Until then, being out was still an issue for those of us who weren't civil attendants. Dane had a plan, though, and we were behind her, whatever it was. Quigley manned his position as navigator, albeit reluctantly; Dane had pulled him away from a connection he was making with Natyli, interrupting their conversation about "expendables" and those without a purposeful, worthy life.

Dane drove with a purpose, taking us more than ten blocks out of the way in order to circumnavigate the Halloween procession, to a neighborhood I recognized from earlier that night. To the right was the home of Bethany, the young girl with the crowd of mourners. The house looked so peaceful in the dawn.

Just ahead was the residence of the daughter and her depressed mother, Diana. Their house was cold and repellent, like a foreclosure or a condemned building. Dane stopped the van in front of it.

"What are we doing here?" asked Quigley.

"Something I should have done," Dane replied. "Something better."

She told her partner to follow her, and she instructed the rest of us to wait. We five scattered to any window we could for a better vantage point to whatever was going to happen outside.

Dane and Quigley approached the darkened doorstep, and Dane knocked on the door. When there was no answer, she pounded on it. Some minutes later, a light came on, and the meek daughter answered. We couldn't hear the conversation, but body language told us everything.

The more Dane spoke, the more tense and the more animated she became. Quigley hung back, looking around agitatedly; he clearly did not want to be there. And the young woman's shoulders slumped in a way that said she wished she hadn't answered the door.

Then they were done.

The woman closed the door and turned out the light. Quigley started back toward us in a hurry. But Dane emerged from the shadow of the house slowly, Natyli's gun in her hand. It had been tucked into Dane's jeans since the party. She raised it and aimed at Quigley's back. Though we had all seen Natyli unload the weapon, the five of us jumped out of the van to intervene. Quigley, confused by our behavior, turned to Dane, saw the gun, and jumped for cover behind us with a *mmrp!*

"Dane, what happened? What's wrong?" Ben asked.

"You gave her *capsules*," she said to Quigley, ignoring Ben, "didn't you?"

"I helped her," Quigley answered. "It was what she wanted."

"You're nothing but a damned reaper!" Dane made attempts to move around and between us to get closer to him.

"It was her choice!"

"Her choice, not yours. It's not for you to decide! If one of us is expendable, then we all are! All of us! Why don't you just kill us all?" Dane cried with such ferocity that saliva foamed at her lips. She was rabid. "You're no better than the rest of them! You're finished! Get out of here! Get out of here!"

Quigley was on the other side of the van, peering through the passenger window and the nonexistent windshield. "Go where? You expect me to just—*mmrp*—walk?"

"No, I expect you to run! Run, reaper, run!"

Quigley didn't run, but he did move quickly out of there, up the street, away from Dane as she finally got around us and circled the van. She stood and watched as the man who had made her see colors distance himself from her until he took the next corner and left our sight.

Dane tempered herself, calmed her breathing, and wiped her face of the tears and sweat and spit.

Ben went to her side and asked exactly what we were all thinking. "What now?"

* * *

Dane soon had a new plan. This one involved trading the FCO van for a less conspicuous mode of transportation. Zac suggested his father's truck.

"You said you moved it, right?" he reminded Ben. "Where did you move it to?"

Ben directed Dane to a facility that used to rent vehicles for moving; the business was now abandoned, with a fleet of trucks left behind.

"It should still be there," Ben told her. "I passed by it a few days ago."

We arrived in a matter of minutes. Samuel's truck was parked, hidden in plain sight, on a lot with a dozen similar-looking trucks. The rusty, cracked wheel wells, the oxidation in the hood's finish, and the frayed, balding tires masked the old moving van's glory days of roadside assistance and clandestine sermons. Still, the truck looked in better shape than the FCO van, and it started like a champ. The truck had a narrow pass-through connecting the cab to the rear cargo area, allowing little visibility into the back. It would be easier for the rest of us to hide, and with her credentials, medical pack, and a story about the truck being an older model FCO vehicle, Dane was confident she could get past any checkpoint—more confident than the rest of us, anyway.

By then, the curfew had lifted. I looked out the pass-through and front window and saw the streets were filling up, so to speak, with activity. We approached a checkpoint; Dane hollered back for us to stay down and keep quiet.

The idle of the engine made it difficult to hear the exchange between Dane and the soldier. I did catch an unusually sweet tone from her and an agreeable response from the noncom, who, fortunately, it seemed was a young, het male; Dane could tantalize as easily as she could strong arm. Then I heard him asking about the truck's dilapidated condition. Dane explained how the agency she worked for was reluctant to invest in newer vehicles. They laughed at something I couldn't discern, and we were soon lumbering along again in the emerging morning light. We were south of Market Street, heading to the site of the previous night's Fallout.

In the dawn, the neighborhood wasn't as foreboding as the night before, yet it wasn't inviting, either. Also, the school where The Fallout had been wasn't as far from the checkpoint as it had first seemed. We quickly arrived to find the area busy with police activity. With the perimeter of the school taped off, hazmat clothed detectives and officers moved from one classroom to another while forensic teams carried items of evidence down to the street and into awaiting cargo vans. *What an expensive venture hosting a fallout party must be*, I thought. As soon as we got close enough, an officer halted our vehicle and approached; Dane turned off the motor and readied both her credentials and her story.

"I'm here to pick up some bodies," she said. "I was told they were somewhere around this playground."

"Haven't seen any," said the officer. There was nothing casual about his speech or demeanor; he was serious about his job, but not quite serious enough to find Dane's unconventional vehicle suspicious.

"What happened here?" Dane asked, feigning interest.

"It looks like some people had a little too much of the wrong kind of fun last night," answered the officer. His response had a puritan air about it. Did his training involve learning to distinguish between "right" and "wrong" types of fun? Or was he passing judgment through his own personal ideology? Either way, his manner indicated the us vs. them attitude to which the partygoers at Natyli's had so adamantly expressed their objections.

"But like I said, ma'am, we haven't seen any bodies," he added.

"You mind if I look around?"

Dane was told to park a safe distance up the street (safe from what, exactly?) and not cross the police barriers in her search for the alleged bodies. She stopped the truck so that it faced the playground. There wasn't room enough for five heads to squeeze into the opening of the pass-through, but that didn't keep all of us from peering forward out the windshield, watching Dane as she searched the area.

The jungle gym–cardboard igloo was as depressing a

sight as Ben had described it, especially knowing a woman and her four children had resided there. Cardboard, warped and stained from rain, was woven within the bars of the jungle gym, along with ragged, grimy remnants of patterned blankets and faded sheets. Though I never got close to it, I imagined it reeked of cold, musty dampness.

We were about a half block away from the playground. Dane cautiously approached the domed structure. She spoke to whoever might be within as she knelt down at its entrance. She waited, put her head inside, then stood and looked in our direction. She shook her head to tell us that no one was there. She searched the vicinity, checking inside and behind a nearby dumpster, and then started back toward the truck. To her right, workmen were busy unfolding the collapsed fencing of the makeshift parking lot while officers took inventory of the entrapped automobiles.

Dane slowly drove around the adjacent neighborhoods, but there was no sign of life. After a half hour, she pulled over, and we sat in silence.

"What now?" Ben asked her once again.

"What is it you're trying to do?" I asked her.

Dane leaned forward against the steering wheel, her head cradled within her hands. After a moment, she said, "I want to do something more than put people out of their misery. I thought I could find that woman with her children and move them out of here or help them somehow."

Lucy crawled into the pass-through to sit beside Dane.

"I've got an idea," she said, and before Dane could object to her presence in the cab, Lucy shared the nightmarish experience that had led to her damaged face. It wasn't easy for her to talk about, but Lucy was determined. She had a plan of her own now.

For a few minutes, Dane considered Lucy's story. Then she asked her, "What motel on the wharf were you in?"

"The Holiday Inn."

* * *

We left the restricted zone, traveled along Van Ness Avenue to a checkpoint at Bay Street, and re-entered it. Dane's story to explain Lucy in the front seat with her—that she was an intern along for an observation ride—was her worst yet, but it worked. Upon a concrete wall that lined the sidewalk to our left was written:

EGOCENTRIC SUFFERING CREATES MARTYRS OF DOOM,

WHILE SELFLESS SUFFERING IS A WASTE OF TIME

Dane slowed down to read. I asked Ben and Zac about it, and suddenly, they were both in the front seat, crowding in between Lucy and Dane.

"What the hell?" Dane complained to them.

"That's not one of Dad's," Zac said.

"It's too long and wordy," added Ben. "Dad kept his short and memorable."

"That's right," agreed Zac.

"And 'martyrs of doom'? What does that mean? It's stupid."

"Then who wrote this?" I wondered.

Zac shrugged.

Ben answered, "We don't know."

The Holiday Inn only four blocks away, Dane pulled the truck over and stopped. The plan was vague at best: get as many of the drugged, sexually abused captives as possible out of the motel and into the back of the truck.

"How did you get out?" Dane asked Lucy.

"Well, I just left, really," she answered. "It was a fluke of circumstances. They had forgotten to give me my nightly dose. I was hurting bad for it, but I was also a lot more coherent, and they happened to give me a customer who was so drunk he could barely walk. He fell asleep on top of me. I pushed him to the floor and found the door ajar and let myself out of the room. No one was patrolling the hall at that moment, so I ran to the stairwell. Next thing I knew, I was in the alley. So I ran. I was naked and it was cold, but I kept running."

There wasn't the "sheer aggression" Shel had alluded to in his version on the rooftop, but what she'd done was still powerful. Lucy went on to explain that the girls and boys, women and men, as many as four to a room, were only held on one floor, the top floor. The remaining rooms below were residences.

"There's only one person patrolling the floor at any one time," Lucy told us.

"We just need to get up to that floor and bring them

down to the truck," said Zac. "I could go in—as a customer—and then go down the stairwell and let the rest of you in. Unless the door is alarmed."

"It wasn't," said Lucy. "They may have fixed that, though. You're going to need cash to get in—at least a couple hundred."

"This isn't a game, Zac," warned Dane.

"I know that. That's why I want to do it."

All of us dug into our pockets and collectively produced one hundred and thirty-seven dollars. Lucy shook her head. "It might be enough, or it might not and you'll be thrown out."

"Well," said Zac as he gathered the cash, "if it doesn't work, we'll just have to come up with another idea."

His cocky self-confidence became infectious, and soon we all felt we could make it happen. I chimed in with my own idea.

"A distraction would help, don't you think?" I was thinking of how everyone at Natyli's party was interested in talking to me, someone from the outside. In the same way, I could enter the motel "looking for a story" and draw their attention toward me rather than anything that might be going on elsewhere.

Dane thought it was too dangerous, but the others agreed it was good idea.

There was one last detail. "What do we do about whoever's patrolling the floor?" asked Ben.

"He'll have access to all the rooms," said Lucy.

"I'll take care of him," said Shel. His voice echoed a vindictive tone from the back of the truck, as though whoever patrolled the rooms was personally responsible for what had happened to Lucy.

Dane took Natyli's gun from her jeans once again. "This will come in handy, too. It sure scared the crap out of Quig."

"What if this guy is not easily intimidated?" Ben asked.

"You heard Shel. He'll take care of him," replied Dane.

The murmur of a bitter laugh came from the back of the truck.

*   *   *

It was easy to imagine a time when the Holiday Inn on the corner of Columbus and North Point was fresh and inviting, a soothing sight for weary travelers—not extravagant, but clean, simple respectability. It was easy to imagine because that was the way it looked as I approached along a street entrance designed more to accommodate automobiles than pedestrians, yet still welcoming. I felt as though I were about to check in and start a relaxing weekend getaway in the infamous, romantic city by the bay. I passed the motel's marquee that announced with dark humor:

WELCOME, SHRINERS

AND MARTYRS OF DOOM!

Inside, the lobby was bright—sparkling, even—with touches of marble and polished trim. While the leafy, swirled pattern of the aged carpet was barely discernible, it was clean. A fair number of people—more than I'd expected at that time of the morning—lingered about. There was a well-dressed concierge and a pair of impeccably uniformed desk clerks primed and alert at their respective stations. An equally well-attired gentleman stood at the bellhop counter, who, by his physique, looked more like a bouncer.

There was no hint of the seedy, heinous environment Lucy had told us about. I wondered for a moment if I was in the right motel, and I feared that perhaps the girl with the damaged face had made it all up—a psychotic hallucination as a result of a bullet grazing her frontal lobe.

"Hello! How are you this morning?" the concierge said to me. His perky welcome contrasted the unhealthy hue of his complexion. "What can I do for you?"

All eyes were on me suddenly. I relaxed and thought about how I was there to do exactly what I was in the city to do. Nothing had to be fabricated. "My name is Aaron Garret. I'm a writer with the *Sound*, and I'm here in the city doing a story on life under quarantine."

My statement didn't get the response I was expecting. The concierge's cheery manner abated, and the bellhop-bouncer was immediately at my side with an enormous hand upon my shoulder. He pushed me down into a cushy armchair, not so that I would be comfortable, but so that he would have an advantage over me, as though his immense size wasn't enough. The concierge stood partly next to him and partly behind him, glaring at me.

"Why are you here? Who sent you?" the concierge asked, his manner now one of interrogator.

I explained again, with a little more detail, about how I had arrived to the city two days prior from Seattle to conduct interviews. I felt I was once again facing soldiers at a checkpoint, needing to prove I was legitimate and official. I reached for my papers. They were gone! At some time in the previous eight hours, my documents had fallen from my jacket. I searched other pockets.

"Thtop! Be thtill!" the bellhop-bouncer said, grabbing my arms. His childlike lisp made him nearly unintelligible.

"Don't move!" said the concierge.

"I'm looking for my papers," I told them. "I have identification."

"He hath a brathlet. Ith green."

"You're risking your life," doubted the concierge, "to write about us?"

I looked around at the other colors in the room; there were a few greens, but mostly oranges. And there were a couple of people, standing upright and mentally coherent, with a red glow around their wrist.

Before I could speak in my defense, everyone was on his or her phone or tablet, running a search on my identity. Fortunately for me, the federal Internet lockdown was easy to circumvent.

One woman stepped forward and showed her handheld to my interrogators. "Look," she said, "there he is." She had the *Sound*'s site on her screen, with my staff bio and photo in view. Others admitted to finding the same.

"Thith lookth legit. I think he'th being thtraight with uth."

The concierge's initial pleasant demeanor returned, and with a beaming smile, he said, "My name is Chicken, and this is Rudy. What is it that you would like to know?"

I hadn't prepared any questions. *But*, I thought, *I don't really need any*. "I want to hear your stories, about how you live here, day to day."

That was all it took. As with the guests at Natyli's party, Chicken and Rudy's desire to share their experience with anyone who would listen bordered on desperation. The others there, too, stayed in the lobby to listen and share. I sat in my comfortable seat, like a tribal elder with the community gathered before him, hearing one unfortunate tale after another. It soon became a childish contest of one-upmanship. Whose circumstances were the worst?

At Natyli's, there had been an air of resentment and cynicism. Yet, in the lobby of the Holiday Inn, their narratives had a kind of pride about them, bordering on arrogance, an attitude that said, *We made our mark! We chose the outcome of our lives! We fought the establishment and won!*

They *had* fought, in what became the worst riot in a taut chain of many, and whether or not they'd truly "won" was a matter of perspective. At the forefront of the unrest had been a man by the name of J. T. Cole, considered either a revolutionary or a homicidal cultist, often compared to Che Guevara or David Koresh. By that description alone, you might have expected Cole to be an intensely handsome man with a hard jawline, a stabbing glare, and a trustworthy smile, someone others would easily follow.

Instead, right there in the lobby, the man who approached to introduce himself from the back of the small group at my feet was gentle, with soft features and a smooth, toneless physique. He had no smile to trust or find suspect with. He was emotionally ambivalent, as though neither depression nor enthusiasm were part of his genetic makeup. He was *the* J. T. Cole.

"I have friends in Seattle," he said as we shook hands, an orange bracelet snug upon his plump wrist. "They live near Greenlake, I think it's called."

"That's a nice area," I replied. What I was thinking, however, was that someone must have called him. While I was sitting there hearing stories, he had gotten word about me, and he was not going miss the chance for publicity and the opportunity to promote his cause.

"Have you had breakfast?" he asked, starting toward the restaurant behind us, adjacent to the lobby.

Its tile floor was scuffed and chipped, as traffic worn as the lobby's faded carpet. There were remnants of elegance in the dining area, the simple yet substantial lines of white columns and large arched windows letting in the morning and showing the street outside. There was also an abundance of lush artificial foliage. The group in the lobby followed us into the restaurant. Few wanted to eat; they were only interested in what J. T. Cole might have to say. I, on the other hand, was interested in both—breakfast and conversation with a cult hero.

It was then that I saw Zac, with his cocky strut, enter the motel. He approached the check-in counter, and I hoped he wouldn't overdo it and attract suspicious, undue attention. It was discomforting to see the desk clerk, a boney woman with shiny black hair and too much mascara, give such cordial customer service, knowing what it was she was selling. From his pocket, Zac removed the cash we had all contributed and placed it on the counter. The clerk gave a playful frown at what must have been a less-than-average amount of money but did not hesitate to scoop all of it into her hand and close the sale. Then with an infectious smile—elated to send the customer off to indulge in any number of unwanted, unspeakable acts upon another person—she directed Zac to elevators at the end of the lobby. When he was out of her sight, she took the phone in front of her, most likely to call the top floor to let them know they had a customer.

J. T. Cole informed me I should order an omelet and avoid any of the questionable meat products. For himself, he ordered a bowl of fruit and a side of toast. I went with the Greek omelet.

What I knew of J. T. Cole barely filled a paragraph. He

had been living an ideal life—running a successful law firm, married with two children, in the process of renovating a hundred-year-old Nob Hill Victorian—when his wife, son, and daughter contracted the Omega, and he was found to be the carrier. Even so, he became the first to speak out against quarantining the city, citing copious civil rights violations. He was an effective orator and soon accrued a zealous following. It was they who fought the police and military. Cole was lionized, and his words "Free to live…Free to die" became their mantra. And when Cole made the statement "We know it's over for us. All we want now is to quietly fade away," they became known as the Fades.

To an outside observer, the result was a contradiction. The Fades won the right to live and die as they pleased, within the confines of a federally enforced quarantine, restricted to a specific area of the city. Yet, for them, it was a victory. "What's important," Cole had said in numerous interviews, "is that *we* chose where we'll live and eventually die. We know we're a health hazard, and we don't want to hurt others. We know this thing will kill us all sooner or later. But until that day, it will be our choice."

Although limited to the neighborhoods of North Beach and Fisherman's Wharf, they were given autonomy to live as they pleased. Like the zoo, it became a city within a city. I looked out the restaurant's picture window and saw an otherwise idyllic city scene unfolding in the morning light. Unlike neighborhoods south of Market, people on the street appeared productive, happy that they had something to do and someplace to go.

"You've been here how many days?" Cole asked me.

"Just a couple," I said.

"And what have you learned?"

That was not something I had yet considered, so I said the first thing that came to mind. "Living really shouldn't be this hard."

There were hums of agreement from our audience, but Cole remained void of expression, as though he hadn't heard me. Then he said, "What about death? Should it be hard?"

This time I thought about it, but I didn't have an answer. "I don't know."

"Life should be interesting, with challenges to make it worthwhile, don't you think? And when you're done, you're done. It's dying that should be easy."

He paused as our food was placed in front of us. He carefully laid his napkin on his lap, organized his silverware, and selected the spoon. He scooped a mouthful from his fruit bowl and slowly savored it before swallowing. After meticulously spreading his butter, he did the same with his toast.

"The problem with the world today is that it's all upside down, isn't it?" Cole continued. "We have easy, pampered lives, and it's just become so hard to die."

He took a few more bites of food and saw that I didn't quite get his point.

"How's the omelet?" he asked.

"One of the best I've ever had," I admitted.

"That illustrates what I'm saying. I think you notice what other people miss. Like a good omelet. It's become our nature to desperately cling to life so that we never really appreciate the moment, and we vehemently resist death when it finally comes along. Our medicine and health care are nothing more than life-support systems, aren't they? We don't need to live longer, just better. Death is inevitable; we should let nature take its course."

"You don't have to resist. There's suicide."

"Unnatural."

"Euthanasia?"

"Only when you've got one foot in the grave. And then there's still a swamp of paperwork to wade through, isn't there?"

He made me think of Samuel Elliot's own blunt, slightly esoteric point of view, as much an inspiration as it was unclear. We finished our breakfast while the others around us began to order their own. We talked about Seattle; he wanted to know about where I lived, my favorite places to eat. Then he told me of other countries he had visited: Japan, New Zealand, Argentina. I confessed I had not been anywhere outside the continental United States.

"Now, that's disappointing, to never experience another culture" was Cole's response.

I shrugged, a little embarrassed, and finished my

omelet. I tried to change the subject. "Do you live here at the motel?"

"My place is a block away. I come here to be around people."

"I've always been a loner myself," I said.

"I imagine many writers are," Cole replied.

Our conversation started to take such a casual tone that, for a moment, I forgot why I was there and what was happening on the floors above us. I was suddenly reminded, though, as a young woman went running naked through the lobby from one of the elevators. Her eyes burst of terror. Her greasy hair and skin glistened as she zoomed past Rudy and out into the street, where she ran with no other purpose but to get away.

"What's going on?" Cole inquired at the commotion in the lobby. He caught sight of the woman without clothes sprinting past the restaurant window and into the distance. He stood to gain a better look. "What the hell is that?"

The surprise and concern of everyone there was so genuine that I wondered if, perhaps, they had any idea of the horrors that took place on the top floor of that motel.

*   *   *

With a toothless smirk and long unwashed hair, an unshaven man in a wheelchair met Zac as he got off the elevator. The halls were dimly lit, and the odors of cigarette smoke, urine, sweat, and Simple Green made Zac nauseous. As he and the others would describe it, the scene was exactly opposite from the bright, friendly atmosphere of the lobby. "It embodied the sleaziness I was expecting from the moment I entered the motel," Zac explained.

The wheel-chaired host immediately zoomed up to Zac, stopping an inch from his shins. "What do you want?" he demanded.

Isn't it obvious? Zac thought to himself? "I paid downstairs. They told me to come up here," he said.

"You're stupid enough to be police. Are you a cop?"

"No, I'm not."

"What do you want, moron? Girl, boy? Black, yellow, pink? Young, old?"

The most rancid breath came from his host's mouth that Zac had to step back, only to stumble into the elevator doors behind him. "A young...um...Asian girl would be fine," Zac answered.

The host nodded in approval, spun his chair around, and zoomed away. As Zac jogged to keep up, he noticed the chair was reinforced with steel bumpers on all sides, which he guessed—along with the chair's oversize motor—were meant to threaten uncooperative "merchandise" or knock down unreasonable customers. Zac also thought that he wouldn't want to be grabbed by the man's powerful arms.

According to Lucy, doors to the rooms could only be opened from the outside. Once in the room, a customer was stuck until their allotment of time (determined by how much was paid to the desk clerk) was complete. Zac had the idea to slip something—a wedge of cardboard, in this case—between the door and the doorjamb to prevent it from closing before it latched. If it didn't work, he would have to come up with another plan. Nothing was coming to mind as he followed the wheel-chaired thug.

The host abruptly stopped at a room and slid a keycard into the electronic lock. "Here," he said, opening the door and waiting for Zac to enter. "She won't resist if you want to shred her ass."

"Isn't it more fun if they do resist?" Zac said, hoping a little crass humor would earn him favor. It did. The host gave a grotesque smile and a hardy, gurgling laugh as the door closed. Zac slipped his piece of cardboard into place. The door closed, but not all the way.

"Hell, I'll give you an extra five minutes! See you in twenty!" the host shouted. His laughter continued down the hallway, and Zac's stomach turned at the thought that they were becoming pals.

He checked the door to make sure it was secure, or rather, *not* secure. Then he looked over his shoulder and into the room. The only light came from the television and a candle. Curled up in a chair directly in front of the TV, her knees tucked tightly to her chest, was exactly what he'd ordered—a young Asian girl. He guessed Korean. She wore a kimono with a tear at one of the shoulder seams, and she looked deathly tired.

The candle was scented but did a poor job of masking

the multiple layers of distasteful odors. Zac gagged when he took a breath. At the sound, the girl turned to him. She wasn't surprised to see Zac standing there, nor did she seem to care. She stood and allowed the kimono to slip from her naked body. At first, Zac had suspected she was in her late teens, early twenties. But seeing her plump, underdeveloped body, he knew she couldn't have been more than twelve or thirteen. She got on the bed, on her knees and elbows, with her back end pointing toward Zac and her face buried into a pillow.

"No," he told her. "No, I don't want that."

She slumped over to one side, then slid from the bed. On her knees, she reached for his belt buckle.

"No, that's not what I'm talking about," said Zac as he pushed her hands away. "Listen to me, okay?"

She looked at him, but Zac never felt that he had her attention; she was in a vacant, distant stupor. ("She reminded me of Peter's mother," Zac later admitted. "That poor girl. She was so lost. If she wasn't having sex, she had no idea what to do with herself.") Zac tried to explain our plan to her, which was that he would get her and the others out of the motel. She didn't respond. She stood with her robe in hand and wrapped it sloppily around her body, then slumped into the chair and resumed watching television.

Zac left her there and went to the door. He cracked it open and peered out, but could only see a short way down the hall. The wheel-chaired sentinel was not in view. Zac could only hope that he had returned to his post by the elevator and was not still in the hallway, beyond his line of sight. Zac put his head out farther and saw the entire length of the hall. It was clear.

He spied the exit and stairwell behind him and gently, quietly, closed the door. Zac knew the piece of cardboard might slip from the doorjamb and the door would close all the way, but once he and the others overpowered the guard and acquired the access key, it wouldn't matter. The silence of the hall was unsettling, like a crypt. Zac hurried down the hall and wondered whether there really was anyone in the other rooms and if they were even alive.

That same silence made his presence in the stairwell all the more jolting. He knew his steps must have echoed through the entire motel, and he expected to be discovered and caught at any moment. He stopped at the sound of his own anxious breaths. Were they his, or the gasps of unseen watchers? As Zac continued his descent, he kept his nerves in check with the thought that it was another one of his challenges, just another game—but this time with a better purpose, a motive greater than his own fear.

He reached the ground floor, saw signs indicating an alarm system was wired to the door, and recalled what Lucy had said in the van, about how the exit alarm had been disconnected by an angry tenant after a thunderstorm kept setting it off. Zac paused and, for the first time in his life, prayed. "I'd never asked God for anything before," he later told me, "but I begged and pleaded and asked for that system not to be activated."

Zac opened the door to only the sound of his panicked inhalation. No alarm. Nothing. Unless it was now a silent alarm? He held the door and listened for feet thudding down the stairs in a rush or sounds of shouting.

"Zac?" came Dane's voice instead. "Is that you?"

He opened the door wide to see her and the others there. They slipped past him as sudden as the gust of ocean breeze that hit his face. The door closed behind them a little louder than he had wanted and they all froze.

"Sorry," Zac winced.

Again, the silence that followed told him they went unnoticed.

Zac led the way upstairs. Floor by floor, Dane, Ben, Lucy, and Shel followed. I was surprised to hear Lucy had gone with them; it said a lot about her, to return to the source of her nightmares. Zac told her about the girl he had seen in the room.

"She was the only one in there?" Lucy wondered. "That's unusual."

"Maybe business is slow," Zac commented.

"Or dying."

Knowing his twenty minutes was nearly up, Zac had the five of them hurry as fast as they could on tiptoe down the still, empty hallway of the top floor. The last thing he wanted was to face the armored wheelchair in that narrow corridor;

they'd have a much better chance in the elevator lobby. Zac's grotesque host was there, eyeing the elevators and watching the time while humming to himself—just another day at the office for him.

Dane burst around the corner while Ben and Shel ran to either side of him to restrain his arms. He was so stunned at the sight of Dane aiming a gun at his head that he was too late to resist their hold. Expletives flew from his mouth instead.

"Shut up!" Dane snapped and gave emphasis to the weapon she was pointing at him. "Zac, grab the keycard."

Zac had noted in which pocket the card was kept and went right to it. The host struggled, but Ben and Shel together were too strong for him. Zac ran back to the hallway and, with Lucy, hurried to the first set of rooms closest to the lobby; Dane told Ben and Shel to release their captive's arms and go along with the two of them.

"Sit on your hands," Dane instructed the host. Then, with great emphasis, she said, "And know that I *will* shoot if you try anything."

The grisly man in the wheelchair had no idea there were no bullets and every reason to believe she would pull the trigger. "With or without the gun, Dane's intense level of purpose was scary," Ben told me later. "I'm glad I wasn't on the receiving end of it."

Zac unlocked every door, blocking each one open with whatever he could find—a garbage can, a towel from the bathroom—and hurrying to the next. Lucy, Shel, and Ben followed, each of them entering an open room to lead the occupants out. In the first room Lucy entered, there were two girls about her age, their blonde hair in pigtails and skin so pale they nearly glowed in the dimly lit space. Both cringed at the sight of Lucy but were coherent and responsive to her urgency.

"Put something on," Lucy told them. "Quickly. We're leaving."

Shel found two heavyset Chinese women in the next room. Lucy had explained to us how some were fed better than others, to accommodate customer preferences. Fetishists got whatever they wanted: plump, emaciated, bald, young, old—whatever. At the sight of the open door, both women bolted, almost knocking over Shel, their robes and bodies jiggling as they ran. Lucy caught them in the hallway and instructed them to wait by the stairwell at the other end of the floor.

Shel heard Ben call for help. In the next room, he found him backing away from a bed where a large man lay naked with a small boy.

"I told you to get the fuck out of here!" the man screamed at Ben.

The boy was lying flat on his stomach, tense from pain and convulsing from crying, with blood all over his backside, between his cheeks, and the inside of his thighs. The man was lying on his side, looking over his shoulder at Ben. At the sight of the blood, Shel didn't allow the man to turn over any farther. He thrust a knee into his back, punched him several times in the back of the head, and pushed his face into the headboard. The man was twice Shel's size but struggled without effect from a defenseless position.

"Get them out of here!" Shel ordered Ben.

There were two more boys sitting in a corner of the room, watching in wide-eyed terror. Ben slipped a robe around the one on the bed and urged all three to follow him out of there. But the two in the corner were reluctant to move as Shel and the large man wrestled. All his weight pushing into the man's back and head, Shel grabbed a portion of sheet with his free hand and wrapped it around the man's neck. He nearly lost control as he released the man's head to take the sheet in both hands, but regained it as he pulled the fabric taut with everything he had. The man's arms flailed behind him, and his legs kicked desperately for leverage. Then he blacked out and went limp; Shel immediately released the sheet.

Breathing heavy and pouring sweat, Shel saw that Ben and the boys weren't moving. "The bastard's unconscious, not dead," he explained. "He'll wake up soon with a headache."

Ben urged the boys to follow him, and they left the room. Shel hesitated, making sure the man was still breathing and that he really would wake up. *Not that he deserves to*, he thought to himself.

There was more of the same in the other rooms, just different ethnicities and ages. In a room at the end of the hall was a woman in her eighties. Zac soon had all the doors on one side of the floor open and was moving quickly to the other half. Dane saw him speed by the lobby from the corner of her eye; she wasn't going to take her attention off her wheel-chaired captive, who, still sitting on his hands, seethed as he watched the terrified and drugged children, teens, and adults he had once lorded over herd past him.

Shel was ready to deal with any other clientele whose activities were disrupted, but no one put up a fight like the first. Instead, they hid behind chairs, covered themselves in shame, or denied any wrongdoing. (One of them stated he didn't even know there was someone else in the room. "I came out of the bathroom, and there she was!") In the end, the abusers looked as pathetic and damaged as the abused. Shel closed the door on each, locking them in their rooms.

"Oh, God!" cried Zac from down the hall. All but Dane hurried to where he was—in a room with four girls, the oldest not more than seven or eight. Each of them was comatose from drugs, starvation, or shock, or all three.

"We've got to get them to a hospital," said Lucy.

"What is it? What's happening?" Dane called out.

Zac appeared in the lobby, a child in his arms. "Four little girls," he told Dane. "This one's probably six years old. I think there's one even younger."

In her revulsion and disbelief, Dane looked over her

shoulder to see up the hallway. It was the split second her captive needed to slip a hand out and hit his control throttle. The wheelchair shot forward. Zac put a hand out to push Dane aside, but it was too late. One of the steel bumpers caught her in the shins, throwing her forward onto the host. He held her in a death hug with one massive arm while the other tried to pry the gun from her.

Zac handed his child to Shel and rushed to Dane's aid. With Herculean strength, Zac took the wheelchair from behind and tipped it to one side, tumbling Dane and her aggressor to the lobby floor. They rolled over on top of each other.

Then the gun went off!

"The bang was so sharp and sudden," Zac said later, "I wasn't even sure of what I'd heard until I saw the smoke and heard that creep screaming, 'You bitch! You shot me!' Then I saw the blood on the carpet."

Shel knew exactly what had happened. "Oh, shit! We forgot the one in the chamber!" he said with an uncomfortable laugh. "There's always one in the chamber!"

The gunshot drew the attention of everyone in the hallway. They froze where they were and glared in the direction of the elevators. A few ventured for a closer look. What they saw was Zac pulling Dane from the weakened grip of the crippled host, whose legs were bent in lifeless, unnatural positions beneath him, and the top half of his body writhed in pain. And blood, lots of blood. One of the heavyset women saw it and began to scream. Then the rest of them screamed, in a chain reaction of panic.

"We've got to get out of here!" shouted Shel.

Zac stood but Dane stumbled back against the wall and fell to the floor. "I think my shins are fractured," she cursed. "I can't stand up!"

Zac gave the keycard to Ben with instructions to open the rest of the rooms. He then put the capsized wheelchair upright and lifted Dane into it. She took the throttle in hand, he stood on the solid-steel rear bumper, and down the hall they shot. The chair's motor had a ridiculous amount of power; Dane had to be careful not to plow down the others.

Panic was rampant, and every door that Ben unlocked only added to it. Those within, having heard the commotion outside the rooms, were bursting to escape. A girl, naked and greasy, took off in the opposite direction, toward the elevators. Zac hopped off the chair and chased after her.

He caught up with her at the elevator, where she was frantically pushing the down button. When she saw the bleeding, dying form of the host, she went into a frenzy. She lashed out at Zac, kicking and clawing at him. He tried to get closer, but it was like consoling a wild animal. The elevator doors opened, and she leapt inside. Zac didn't dare get in with her.

He ran back down the hall, shouting, "Hurry! We're going to have company!"

The pandemonium escalated even further. Bigger

escapees knocked down smaller ones. The old woman was pushed aside. A few ran back into their open rooms to hide; they were not going to leave their false solace—not willingly, anyway.

Against Zac's protest, Dane zoomed the wheelchair into each of those rooms, forcing anyone she could find into the chair with her and speeding out. Zac made sure to close the doors after them so there was no getting back in. By the time Dane reached the stairwell, she had seven people piled upon her lap.

"We're going down the stairs," Lucy explained to the hysterical group. "We have a truck waiting."

The group pushed forward. There were more than thirty in all, and into the stairwell they poured. The youngest, unconscious girls were carried, and one of the more cognizant men assisted the old woman. Zac and Dane were last, him lifting her onto his back. He made the precarious descent as quickly as he could behind the others.

"We made so much noise in that stairwell," Ben told me later, "it's a wonder we didn't wake the entire motel. But we made it to the bottom and outside without any conflict."

It was light out. There was activity on the streets and sidewalks. As Lucy had said, the truck was waiting. In the light of day, its decrepit appearance was even more apparent. The rust, the peeling paint, and the dark abyss of the cargo area must have been an unnerving sight to the captives. And who knows how long it had been since any of them were outside? The moment they stepped into the morning's bracing air, most of them ran, tearing off in every direction, their bare feet smacking across the cold concrete and asphalt; their excited, terrified cries shattered the quiet and drowned the shouts of Dane and the others for them to stop.

There was no chance of collecting them. The few who remained—the young boy with the bloody back end, the old woman and the man, and the four unconscious girls—were loaded into the back of the truck. Zac laid Dane there, too, as there was no way she was able to drive. How they were going to get out of the restricted area was the least of his concern. All he knew was that Dane and the others needed immediate medical attention.

*   *   *

Minutes after the greasy woman ran through the lobby and past the restaurant window, we saw more women and children running pell-mell away from the motel.

J. T. Cole and others kept asking, "What the hell is going on?"

When I noticed Rudy, the bellhop-bouncer, enter one of the elevators, I realized it was time to make my own exit. I crossed the street to the other corner, and Zac pulled up with his father's truck. I climbed into the cab with him. The others were in the back.

I knew it wasn't the best time for details, but I had to ask, "How did it go?"

"It wasn't pretty," Zac replied. "Dane's legs might be

broken, and we've got some children who may be even worse off than that."

Every time we hit a bump, Dane cursed in pain; otherwise, the truck's cargo was quiet. In the silence, I thought about how I had a plane to catch that afternoon and how much I wanted to stay. There was so much to do there that was more important than my little story. I wanted to be a part of that city's resurrection; I knew, someday, it would all be better. It had to be. I expressed my feelings to the others.

"You've got to get back to Seattle," Zac said.

"Your story is going to fuel the city's rebirth!" Ben called out.

"You can always come back," said Lucy.

"When are you supposed to meet your escort to the airport?" Zac asked.

"Three hours," I answered.

"That's plenty of time to drop them off at the hospital and get you to the house!"

I knew they were right. I had to finish my assignment. And I hadn't yet interviewed Mrs. Elliot.

SOMETHING BETTER

"If there's ever to be an end of days, I think we're living it now, here, in my lifetime" was Ben's first blog post. And one morning during my visit, Dane commented, "There's all kinds of sickness out there."

On my flight home, I couldn't help but wonder if what was happening in San Francisco wasn't a microcosm of our planet's history of the past century. From planes being flown into skyscrapers to madmen gunning down children in schools; from gang wars in our backyards to countless genocide around the planet; from the global horrors of the Third World War and the North Asia Conflict to the personal challenges against our faith that toppled so many churches from grace—hell, we've been careening toward the end for decades.

My return to Seattle was anything but a homecoming. Upon arriving, I was isolated to a hospital room for the first forty-eight hours and run through a greater barrage of tests than I had had prior to my departure five days earlier. Getting past any one of the military checkpoints had been far less challenging, even with the eventual loss of my papers.

The exams were both physical and psychological. I don't know what kind of trauma it was thought I had undergone, but I was treated like a soldier returning from the war in East Africa. However, the results of the myriad of tests were satisfactory, and I was released with a clean bill of health. Then came a whole new gamut of social trials.

People kept their distance from me at work, and not in subtle ways, either; I was told by more than one coworker not to enter their cubicle or office, as though that would keep them safe. The senior editor asked me to stay at least five feet away from anyone "as a courtesy," and one woman put up a barrier of yellow duct tape ten feet from her desk. It looked like the scene of a violent crime investigation.

Oh, sure, everyone was pleasant enough, doing their best to mask the blatant fear of me and what I may have brought into the safe haven of their workplace. I did what I could, *as a courtesy*, not to be a threat. But by the end of the first week, I'd had enough. I went about my work, disregarding comfort zones, forcing others to clear a path for me; those I had once considered friends stepped aside as though I were a leper. The next week, I was given my own office from which to work. The week after that, it was strongly suggested I telecommute. A few weeks later, I was let go from the *Sound* for an entirely different matter.

It's now been ten months since my three days in San Francisco. Recently, I've been corresponding with Nikki Chin, who had called me after reuniting with her mother and sister, and we've exchanged numerous e-mails. She, too, has been shunned and faced prejudices.

"Before my arrival to Sacramento," she wrote, "my mother was pressured to move when her neighbors found out where I had been for the last two years. Since then, I've twice made the mistake of sharing my experience in San Francisco, and we had to move again. Now I lie, or don't say anything at all. What's next, having an omega symbol burned into my forehead?"

"I want one on my ass," I wrote back. "I wouldn't have any problem showing it to those who need to see it."

This discrimination was universal—the quarantine of San Francisco stretched far beyond its city limits. I found as many as ten domestic airports that banned incoming flights from Northern California, seven more that prohibited air travel from anywhere in the state, and a dozen foreign cities with severe restrictions on the United States as a whole.

Nikki confessed a longing to return to the Bay Area, and I had to agree. "It really is more hopeful than hopeless," she wrote. "It always has been. Remember when we went to the reopening of that fish place? Ben told me new businesses are starting up every week. It's become a kind of renaissance. Now there's talk of lifting the quarantine—at least for parts of the city."

My desire to return to San Francisco prompted me to present my editor with the idea of a follow-up story. But Charles Baxter, founder and owner of the *Sound*, had another plan for me—termination. "Your choice to participate in a number of questionable activities," he explained to me in a formal letter, "has put my business, and me personally, in a precarious legal situation."

He referred, specifically, to my entering the restricted areas of the city, of which he was in dispute with the federal government and State of California. (Not to mention how we smashed a checkpoint on Van Ness in our escape from the Holiday Inn. Zac had had enough of playing games and drove his father's truck through the barrier, nearly taking out two guards in the process.) In violation of World Health Organization codes, I was deemed a "severe health risk." During the five long weeks of litigation, I was once again isolated—*imprisoned*, actually—and put through more tests.

Baxter Enterprises, taking responsibility for my actions, paid the steep fines. There was an onslaught of civil lawsuits—primarily from the proprietors of the Holiday Inn for my involvement in "the invasion of their privacy" and "the unwarranted charges made against their establishment and the many who reside within." Fortunately, the judge saw through the absurdity of the suits and enthusiastically threw them out of her court—but not before the great financial expenditures of all involved parties.

I put my five-week "imprisonment" to good use by

putting together the pieces of my three-day assignment, pieces so large I should have easily stumbled over them in the dark.

First, the suspicious behavior of the old man in front of the zoo and the manner in which outsiders were so strictly kept as outsiders. Zac was right to be nervous about being caught within their community. A well-organized community it was, with its own security force and a self-sufficient means of monitoring their own health—not something you would expect from a random group of homeless. And there was the fact that none of them wore ID bracelets. They were intentionally off the grid and intended to stay that way.

Ben wrote on more than one occasion how the Shepherds of Prophecy were followers of Samuel Elliot's ministry. One entry stated, "Dad talked about how we were the past of things to come. And he would ask of his congregation, 'What kind of future do you want to be responsible for?' But he said that the Sheep Herders, or whatever they call themselves, didn't listen. They didn't get it. He said they were only listening to the voices in their heads."

But who were these Shepherds?

They came from all corners of the scientific and academic communities, with five key members having the greatest influence over their cause: Dr. Martin Ubel, whose dissertation, *Selective Genetics: Correcting Evolution's Mistakes*, was only mildly controversial compared to the experiments he conducted on "aborted" fetuses; Sister Laurel Walker, a professor of theology excommunicated for her harsh criticisms of Christianity as a "spiritually disingenuous and politically manufactured belief system"; Dr. Phinneas Mann, a microbiologist known for experimenting with "mutator alleles" and "forced mutation" of pathogenic microbes; and the biochemist team of Drs. Paula Reid and J. Edward Smith, who were discharged from their positions with the Stanford University Medical Center for their clandestine research and development of drug-resistant bacterium.

It was at the World Peace Summit held in Beijing where these Shepherds first entered the public eye. They spoke out on overpopulation, archaic religious practices, depleted resources, gluttonous governments, and the need for a new world order—*their* new order. I found a photograph of them together in front of the Beijing International Conference Center. One man stood out in the crowd. He was over a foot taller than everyone else, and the thick lenses of his glasses greatly magnified his eyes, just like the first time I'd seen him—the bearded praying mantis peering out at me from inside the zoo's foreboding entrance. The caption under the photo noted him as Dr. Phinneas Mann. Next to him was a woman with gray-streaked hair tied tightly into a bun, and an infectious enthusiasm in her smile—Sister Laurel Walker.

Samuel Elliot had been well aware of the Shepherds' plan, part of which was to clear out the zoo by poisoning the animals and then setting up a secluded camp within its lush walls, where a constant ocean breeze would stave off urban pollution—and other contaminants.

Ben wrote about that night in the zoo with his father:

It was easy to get into the zoo. He knew of a hole made by a gang that had raided it a while back. We crawled through, me dragging a bag of spray paint, and emerged near the tropical forest building. There, he grabbed a ladder from the side of the building, climbed it, and painted, "God Hates Cowards."

He saw the question on my face and said, "I'm trying to correct a wrong. Something I've done. And something that might be done."

We walked the length of the grounds, stopping here and there so he could spray his messages. He said they were warnings. Things like "Surviving Is Not Living" and "Unnatural Behavior Is Failure." Inside the main entrance, along the side of the gift shop, he painted, "Give a Thought to God."

He left a few more as we made our way back past the bear exhibits before slipping back out through the hole. I asked my father what was going to happen. He said he wasn't exactly sure, but it wasn't going to be good. Then he said, "I hope this will fix what I've done."

As we know, it didn't.

The Shepherds of Prophecy took the next step in their plan: avenge the mistreatment of the planet with the release of the Omega virus. Then they would patiently wait for the chaos to pass. They saw themselves personifying Samuel's words, just as it was written upon the gates of the zoo's entrance; they saw themselves as the past, the only past, of the future to come.

The final piece was placed in my lap by Mrs. Elliot during our brief interview on the morning of my departure.

After Zac had dropped off everyone else at the hospital, he took me to pick up my things and talk to his mother. She was out on her morning walk by the time we got to the house; I found her near the muddy mound that was her husband's grave, the trees of the zoo in the background. She wasn't surprised to see me, and she seemed unfazed that her two sons had been gone all night.

"What time does your escort get here?" she asked me.

"In an hour."

"Did you have some breakfast?"

"Yes, I did."

As we talked, she picked up bits of trash that had collected around Samuel's "burial plot." "And did you get your story?"

"Well, we didn't really have our interview, did we?"

"What's important is that someone came here and saw the city with an objective point of view."

"I don't know how *objective* I'm going to be."

Mrs. Elliot smiled. "I think you'll do fine, Aaron."

"I mean, I can't say yet how convinced I am of your

husband's innocence."

"He isn't," she replied quickly. "Not entirely. Samuel was very irresponsible. He was an intelligent, passionate man. He was also a stubborn child who liked puzzles and wordplay. The graffiti he plastered around the city was as much silly fun for him as they were thought-provoking messages for others. He didn't realize until it was too late the power and the consequences of his ideas."

"I got from Ben that he tried to make things right. Is that true?"

"Yes, in his own way. But he should have gone to the FBI. Instead, he thought he could use his words to deter the more radical followers in the same way he had inspired them. They had long decided their intentions, though. Samuel simply became the catalyst for their actions."

Mrs. Elliot bent to grab a piece of rotted cardboard. Her outstretched arm revealed that her bracelet was wrapped with black fabric, its green glow completely covered. I asked her about it.

"It's my small way of protesting what's been done," she said.

"You find the actions of the authorities to be unreasonable?"

"I don't do it for them." She took a few steps along the sidewalk and stopped, directly facing the zoo. "I do it for them. They watch everyone, to protect themselves. They're probably watching us right now."

I looked over and saw only trees and the thick underbrush Zac and I had crawled through. Before I could ask her for specifics, Mrs. Elliot turned and started back to the house.

"There, you have your interview," she said. "Have you got your things together?"

"All but my papers—I seem to have lost them," I told her.

"Then you're stuck here," she replied with another smile. "You're one of us."

My lawyers used what I knew in defense of my case; they argued that I had been "coerced" by the FBI into gathering information for their investigation, which they had yet to follow up on. Mostly to prove me wrong, I thought, federal agents entered the zoo grounds, but found the community indeed populated by the Shepherds of Prophecy, including four of its founders. Dr. Phinneas Mann was not among them. Also captured were ecoterrorists Damascus Shane and Angela Thomas. While the collection of hard evidence proving responsibility continued, I was acquitted of all charges.

What was most important to me, for Mrs. Elliot's sake, was that attention was finally taken off of her husband, Samuel Elliot. In a bold moment, I demanded that the Elliot family be moved to a new location, as they, too, had received threats upon their lives; we were all in danger, I insisted, because of the incompetence of government investigators.

*   *   *

Nikki Chin wasn't the only one to keep in touch with me. Dane sent a letter shortly after I returned home. I wasn't able to say good-bye to her; I had a plane to catch, and she was in the emergency room with two broken legs.

She began by thanking me for my help. "I didn't agree with your coming to San Francisco at first," she wrote. "But I'm glad you did. I think we'll all realize someday that your presence here was instrumental in our transition to move ahead."

She went on to tell me about what happened to her that night at Natyli's party, upon hearing Gorecki's Third Symphony:

"I'd never seen colors to music before. But listening to that piece—there's no descriptive to do it justice, really. My head filled with an immense spiral of green light. At its edge flickered glowing shades of red and lavender that intensified as the singer's voice intensified. I felt as though I were floating underwater, gazing upward to the surface, which was like the sky. And above that, Aaron, was God. And He was touching the water's surface, sending ripples of green and purple across it.

"It wasn't the beauty of the colors, or the splendor of the rippling water that affected me. It was that I actually thought of God. I'd never seen colors to music, and before that night, I'd never given a thought to God. Not really. Yet there He was. I felt his touch. I knew of His presence with all my soul."

I don't know if what Dane experienced was a manifestation of her synaesthesia, or the effects of inhaling several POGO sticks, or if it was truly a religious experience. Perhaps it was all three. But I do know something happened to her. I'll always remember and envy that look of clarity upon her face afterward, and the purity of her mission as she confronted Quigley, telling him, "If one of us is expendable, then we all are!" Would saving any one person make a difference? Before that night, Dane didn't think so. But after God's touch, she believed it would. No, like Samuel, she *knew* it would. And that became her mission and her purpose.

"Death has been in the driver's seat far too long," Dane went on in her letter. "It should be the choice only when there are no more choices. Quigley didn't get that. I think few people do. But it's what Samuel was trying to teach us—that *life* is always first. I know now it's what he meant by his 'three wishes.' He didn't wish for people to die, but for them to strive for life under even the most dire circumstances, to find hope where there isn't any, to not be afraid to live. And in turn, to not be afraid to die, because fear is not God's way.

"I loved Samuel Elliot. They're all a family I never had. I once told you I thought Samuel could've released the virus. I don't know what I was thinking. Sure, he was disappointed in people, and maybe I was a little disappointed in him because I didn't understand everything. But it wasn't in his nature to do such a thing, to harm others."

I think Dane understood more than she realized. Considering Ben's account of his father's assault upon the rude man in the zoo bathroom, the enigma of Samuel Elliot may never be fully grasped.

*   *   *

I also received several e-mails from Ben; he became my firsthand correspondent:

I thought you might like to know what's been happening since you left. There's been a lot of peaceful demonstrations for the quarantine to be lifted—at least partially, if not fully—and it has prompted a few congressmen and women to push for new legislation in that direction.

Of course, Dane doesn't think we should rely on politicians for anything. She says we can only be responsible for ourselves (something my father would have said). However, it was a politician, Mayor Zeng, who helped us out of our trouble with the police and the Holiday Inn.

While her legs are healing, Dane spends her time organizing a plan for a community support system within the FCO. It mostly involves the distribution of experimental drugs and gives patients greater access to in-home care. She explained it as having something to do with giving people a chance to live before they die.

— — —

Zac had an opportunity to leave the city recently but

chose to stay. He didn't give it a second thought. (You can guess that it made our mother very happy.) He's been promoting his own business of bringing fine dining to customers in their own home. He prepares meals for as few as one, as well as catering entire dinner parties. He still works lunches at The Cliff House.

— — —

Our mother has been hosting Bible study groups at home. We've only had one minor incident involving obscenities painted on the front of the house, and the police did give my mother a stern warning about what she was doing to provoke the graffiti. Mother kindly thanked the officers for their concern and sent them on their way. We repainted the house and haven't had any problems since.

Though Peter moved his mother to Boise, Idaho, to live with her sister, Mother talks of finding a bigger house. She hasn't said, but I'm sure it's to accommodate larger study groups and house anyone who might need it.

— — —

Things have not gone well for Drake and Natyli. He's in jail for breaking into a trucking company's warehouse. I don't know what he was going to do there, but Zac said it was part of a challenge given to him by Natyli—and Zac thinks she's the one who made the anonymous tip to the police.

Zac suspects that Natyli wanted Drake out of her life so she could have a new man around. I don't know who he was, but I know her plan backfired when he and some of his friends beat her and raped her repeatedly over the course of a weekend. She was found wandering the streets, her body covered in blood and contusions, and five of her front teeth missing.

— — —

Thanks again for getting us relocated. Our new place is huge, and on clear days, I can see the water. Lucy and Shel have been spending a lot of time with us here. They helped with painting and have attended a few of my mother's study groups. Not so much, I think, for the spiritual guidance, but because they adore my mother and long for the connection and interaction with other people.

One of the cornerstones of my father's ministry was that religion is about bringing people together and defining their culture, not about defining God. I know he would approve of Lucy and Shel attending Bible study—not to study the Bible, but to bond with others. And, in his strange way, he would approve of the series of events, no matter how horrible, which have made the bonding possible.

* * *

Three weeks had passed since I last heard from Ben.

Then I got a call from Nikki. She said Ben had contracted the virus and passed away in a matter of days; he succumbed to the disease so quickly that doctors suspected he had been carrying it for months, slowly breaking down his system until his body finally gave in.

"Dane has taken it the hardest," Nikki told me. "She's been obsessing about when he would've been exposed to contamination. She blames herself, of course. She thinks she brought it into the house. I told her it probably happened when he went into the restricted areas. The Fallout. The motel. She blamed herself for that, too. But does it really make a shred of difference now? He's gone." Her voice cracked, lost to tears and a bad connection.

I was speechless. If I could have thought of anything to say, I would never have been able to get the words out of my mouth. All I could do was think of the young man who had effortlessly carried my luggage at our first meeting, and who had philosophized on the beach overlooking Seal Rock. He had been one surprise after another.

Not long after her call, Nikki sent me a package, at Ben's request. It was all of his journals and a notarized statement giving me permission to use any part of it I wanted. I've been working with an editor to publish all of it, with the proceeds going to the Elliot family. His insights and friendship will forever be invaluable to me.

I regret there was something I hadn't had a chance to give him. Through an online search, I found a byte of the shortwave broadcast of which Zac had made a tape. The broadcast had aired from Quito, Ecuador, but it was originally a recording of their father sent in by a listener in San Francisco to the station. As Ben had said, his father never went to South America. Yet his voice, his words, spanned the world. And it came through loud and clear on my computer:

"We need to find the belief we had before the written word—visceral, primal belief. We need to find the connection we lost long ago—to the earth, to each other, to God—connect in such a way that God permeates everything we do and all that we are, without consciousness. We shouldn't practice belief, like a weekly sermon, it should be lived every day, until it becomes more than belief, until it becomes knowledge and then wisdom. If not, we live with only what is at our fingertips, only for the moment; we stagnate, and then death triumphs.

"This truth came to me as I watched my church burn to the ground. The structure that was turning to ashes beneath the flames was nothing more than a construct by men within which to worship God, like any religious doctrine, but it was not God. It was just a building, and the sacred texts inside were just books. All man-made. And as I gazed upon the smoldering embers, the smoke intertwining with the morning fog, I felt—no, I knew—that God was not any less in the absence of those material things. If anything, God was even greater to me then. It was then my belief became wisdom. And most important, that my wisdom was not meant to be idle."

His words were magnetic, but his voice was common. It wasn't a prophet I listened to, just a man. A man who *knew* there was something to live for, an ideal greater than us for which to strive—and it wasn't found in the constructs of other men. It wasn't in the churches, or the synagogues, or the mosques, or the temples. It wasn't in religion. The Scriptures could all be burned; they were unnecessary.

What Samuel Elliot knew was that we need each other. We need to live knowing none of us are expendable, that being alive is to be most cherished. We need to live—not idly, but actively—as a functioning part of something greater than all of us. He knew hope grows from the idea of something better. And he knew—what Dane had learned and what the Shepherds never understood—that within that idea of something better, we might just think of God.

About the Author

After decades of self-doubt and errant life choices,
Gordon Gravley finally came to finish this, his first novel,
and is now diligently working on his next.
He and his wife currently reside in the
Northwestern United States.

www.ingramcontent.com/pod-product-compliance
Lightning Source LLC
Chambersburg PA
CBHW050610190726
48283CB00007B/2363